REUNION

By Ian Searle

Copyright © 2025 Ian Searle

All rights reserved. No part of this publication may be reproduced or transmitted in any form or by any means, electronic or mechanical including photocopying, recording or any information storage or retrieval system, without prior permission in writing from the publishers.

The right of Ian Searle to be identified as the author of this work has been asserted by him in accordance with the Copyright, Designs and Patents Act 1988

First published in the United Kingdom in 2025 by

The Cloister House Press

ISBN 978-1-913460-88-4

Chapter One

"Good Heavens!" Jim said, "Joe? Joe Morissoni?"

Gemma, who found her husband's habit of checking email messages at breakfast annoying but had grown used to it after so many years, looked up.

"Who is Joe?" she asked. Instantly she regretted asking, but it was too late. Jim continued to stare at his laptop as he explained in the irritatingly vague way of his.

"Joe isn't his proper name," he said. "It's a nickname."

Gemma waited.

"The Morissonis owned a hotel, still do, by the look of it." He turned the screen so that she could see the address and small picture.

"But where is this?" Gemma asked.

"Fallowfield."

"Fallowfield?"

"You remember I went to school there!"

"That was a long time ago, surely?"

Jim frowned. "I suppose so," he said.

"Before I ever met you."

"Yes, it would have been. We moved as soon as I'd taken my A levels. That was, let's think, twenty-five years ago."

"So, why is this Joe person emailing you after all this time?"

"See for yourself." Jim poured himself another cup of tea and waited for his wife to read an emal from a hotelier she had never heard of who lived in a town fifty miles away which she had never visited.

Beneath the formal heading the message began in an unexpectedly informal style.

"Jim, Hi,

I wonder if you remember me. I am Giuseppi Morrisoni whose name you could never remember. You called me J as all our classmates did. Yu may also remember my family owned the Hotel Morisoni in Fallowfield and we were in the same year. The hotel is now mine. In conversation with a couple of people we were at school with and who still live in Fallowfield, we hatched the idea of setting up a Twenty-Fifth Reunion. I have been busy tracking down as many former pupils as I can. I know you left Fallowfield at the time in question, but that is one of the things that would make a reunion so interesting.

We are planning to hold the Reunion here in Fallowfield, of course, but if you, plus your partner/wife would like to attend, you would be welcome to stay at the Hotel Morissoni at half the normal price for the two nights. Further details are attached. Response has been very good, considering we are all 25 years older. We are assured that at least sixty former pupils and partners, as well as one or two former teachers will attend. A newly-appointed Headmaster has also agreed to attend.

It will be fascinating to discover what paths everyone has followed since we all shared a few early years together. Please reply to me at the hotel and I promise we shall make you very welcome.

"Giuseppi (Joe) Morissoni."

"The hotel looks good," Gemma commented. "The pictures of the bedrooms look very pleasant and clean."

"They probably are," Jim said.

"You don't sound very interested. Don't you want to go?"

"No. Why, do you?"

"Yes, it sounds intriguing. I've never been there. I have no memories, like you. It will certainly have changed in 25 years anyway. A couple of days by the seaside at half price, meeting lots of new people – yes, good idea."

Jim was clearly surprised. "You won't know anybody," he said.

"Nor will you. It will be like a party. Well, it is a party, I suppose. I know you went to school with these people but they will surely all have changed a lot since you knew them. It would be interesting to find out what's become of them. Anyway, I would like to go. Fallowfield sounds like an interesting little town."

"OK. I suppose it could be interesting. The hotel looks a lot smarter than I remember it. It's still not exactly cheap."

"Don't be so mean! The standard rate looks quite high, I suppose, but at half price it becomes quite a bargain. Has it occurred to you that your work as an accountant is peaking you were a bit miserly?"

Jim looked at her and careened. "I just like value for money," he said. "I hope the foods good."

"This is new," Jim said. "The road used to lead directly into the town. This bit is completely new. The coast road must bypass the town itself." He negotiated the roundabout. Gemma gave him a little anxious glance. Ever since she had insisted, she would like to take up the invitation, she sensed Jim was less than enthusiastic. She could not think why. Perhaps there were things, secrets, to do with his childhood or school days. He had never said much about his time in Fallowfield, never spoken of any school friends. It had never come up in conversation. Her knowledge of

Jim's past, she realised, began when he arrived in Burshot at the age of eighteen. His father had taken up the headship if the local school, bringing his wife and Jim with him. It had been a traumatic time and Jim said little about it. Gemma was unable to ask too much. She knew the bare facts. Jack, Jim's father, had taken his own life two years after the move. Mrs Granger never recovered from the shock and, after a year spent in a mental hospital had died in her turn. It was at this time that Gemma met Jim. She was completing her qualification in law, about to become a solicitor, dealing with conveyancing. Jim was already on the way to becoming an accountant. One year later they married.

That, Gemma told herself, was nineteen years ago. The two of them were busy with all the usual occupations of the newly-married. They had decided early on they did not want children. They were far too busy building their careers, saving money to buy a house and driven by a need to become financially secure. Such hobbies as they had involved travel on a modest scale. Gemma's parents did not understand or approve of the couple's stated plan to remain childless. This difference grew and resulted in a widening gap. The young Graingers thus became an isolated couple. They did not mind. They were, generally speaking, content within their own bubble. For Gemma this trip to Fallowfield was much like the scores of visits they had made together but, looking again at Jim's face as they headed into the town, she suffered a small pang of disquiet.

A road took them downhill and there, all at once, was the sea. They turned left along a broad promenade. Several hotels lined the road on the left. They overlooked a handsome bay. A short way ahead, beyond the hotels, Gemma could see a wharf. Two sizeable boats were moored there, spick and span. Before she could take in more, however, Jim had swung the car up a small road that led directly to the Hotel Morisoni.

A smart, young girl greeted them at the reception desk. When Jim gave their name, she said, "Oh, Mr and Mrs Grainger! Mr Morrissoni would like to welcome you. He'll be here in a moment."

Mildly surprised, they waited for no more than a moment, then a corpulent man in a light blue suit burst out of a door behind the reception desk. The jacket bulged over a brightly patterned waistcoat. He was smiling widely. Gemma glimpsed a gold tooth as he welcomed Jim and herself, skipping round the desk like a professional dancer and extending a well-manicured hand.

"Jim, Mrs Grainger!" he said. "Welcome, welcome! I'm so glad you could make it. I'll show you to your room. Are those your luggage?"

He picked up the two modest cases and led the way to the lift with the room key the receptionist handed him. "I've put you in Room Number 9," he said. "It has a lovely view of the Bay. I expect you'd appreciate time to recover from your journey. If you wish, you can come down to the bar for tea. The Reunion will be held in the new school hall. I've ordered a minibus to take our guests there and bring them back, so you won't need to drive. Here we are, Number Nine. We can catch up later, if you'll forgive me. I don't think I'd remember you after all this time."

"Whew!" Gemma exclaimed, when he left at last. "So that's Joe!" She sat on the bed. "He's right about the view, anyway." She lay back, remarked the bed was comfortable.

Jim was happy to make a cup of tea in the room, but Gemma insisted they should go downstairs. As usual, she won. The Bar was a large, well-furnished room. It was clear that the hotel was well run and the staff were polite and helpful. There were ten guests sipping tea and eating biscuits or cakes. They all looked up when Gemma and Jim came in.

A round, ruddy-faced man spoke. "This is surprisingly awkward," he said. "Nobody is recognisable after all this time. I'm Toby Chatterton, 'Chatters.' I'm afraid I don't recognise you."

"Jim Grainger."

There was a tiny hesitation, then Toby replied. "Of course! Jim! Good to see you again. Didn't you move asway as soon as you left school?"

"Yes," said Jim. "What about you?"

Gemma was intrigued, as she had expected to be, as the assortment of men, now in their forties, found themselves having to explain who they had become, explain who they were when teenagers, introducing their spouses. But Gemma, watching and listening detected minor things which might be her imagination at work. Jim seemed very reluctant to talk about his leaving Fallowfield. Genna could well understand his reluctance to talk about his father's suicide and his mother's painful, mental collapse and death. He was ready, when asked, to explain his choice of career as an accountant. Gemma helped him by talking about their travels. It was not just Jim's reluctance to talk about himself, however. Gemma had the distinct impression that Jim's schoolfellows, sometimes even their wives, were slightly unwilling to talk to him. She tried discretely to discover if Jim had been especially unpopular at school, but there was no indication that was so.

The tea party broke up and everyone retired to prepare for the evening at the school. Jim did not seem to be enjoying the day. Gemma felt guilty as well as curious. What, she wondered, lay beneath this strange unease? Perhaps it might have been better not to have come. Still, the evening should be enjoyable. Judging by the standard of entertainment provided by Joe Morissoni, the Reunion would be like a splendid Ball. She was glad she had packed her favourite dress.

The hotelier travelled with them in the minibus. "Here we are!" he announced in a cheerful voice as they stopped in front of a fine, brick-built building.

"Where are we?" Jim asked. "This isn't the school."

"Of course! I never thought," said Joe. "The old school was replaced 10 years ago. This is a splendid new place. You'll like it. Follow me." He watched as everybody disembarked, the ladies are shaking up their skirts, then led the way towards the large, glass doors which were manned by smiling helpers. Inside, individual name tags were arranged in alphabetical order. Everyone hunted for his or her name and, suitably identified, they were ushered into the main hall.

The organisers had given a great deal of thought to this celebration. All round the periphery small tables had been set up. Many of the chairs had already been taken. The centre of the hall was left as a space for dancing and, on a platform at one end, a drum kit and two microphones suggested that a band would provide music. Meanwhile each guest was expected to hand his or her nametag to a splendidly attired Toastmaster who called out their names and allowed, clear voice. Beyond that the Toastmaster an elderly man stood and smiled a greeting.

"Good Lord!" said Jim. "It's old Mr Jennings. He used to be Deputy Head. I quite liked him. Very fair."

"Well," said Gemma, "he's neither dark nor fair now." He was quite bald. Jim ignored her, however, waiting for their names to be called so he might speak to the old man.

"Mr James and Mrs Gemma Grainger" the voice boomed. Several heads turned towards them as they moved on to Mr Jenkins.

"Welcome," he said. "It has been a long time. I hope this is proving a pleasant visit. I'd like the chance to chat later."

"That would be nice," Jim said.

"Lovely to meet you, Mrs Grainger," said the old man, but he looked mildly insincere. Maybe she was imagining things, thought Gemma, accepting a glass of wine from a young man who was dressed as a waiter.

The floor was busy as arrivals moved about, welcoming acquaintances. Many guests would probably live in Fallowfield still. Some were reading the name tags to check they were not mistaken as they greeted schoolfellows from more than twenty years ago. Others were introducing their wives and husbands.

A rather rude man introduced Gemma but seized upon Jim, eager to speak to him. Gemma ignored him and found an empty chair at one side of the hall. Within a matter of minutes, she was joined by a jawboned woman wearing a dress which was too tight. She sat down, peered at the name-tag round Gemma's neck, and asked, "Mrs Grainger?"

"Yes," said Gemma., choosing not to elaborate.

"" Are you any relation to Jack Granger?"

"Jack Grainger? No, yes, well, sort of," said Gemma.

"Sort of?"

"My husband's father was Jack Grainger."

"Was? I don't understand," said the woman. She had large teeth, Gemma noticed, and they were discoloured. She was in need of a visit to a hygienist. "Are you saying Jack Grainger is your father-in-law?"

"I never met him," Gemma explained. "He died before I met my husband."

"Oh, I see. That was some time ago, I imagine?"

"About twenty years," said Gemma. She was growing tired of this personal interrogation, but before she could ask questions in her turn, the ill-dressed woman stood up abruptly to say hallo loudly to someone on the next table. As she turned away, Gemma caught a glimpse of her name tag, Farmer.

The Toastmaster's voice announced the arrival of the new Headmaster and his wife. Everyone was asked to find a seat so that the headmaster could welcome everyone. Mr Jenkins would say a few words first. Gemma braced herself for a boring half-hour and took a mouthful of wine. She grinned sympathetically at her husband and was disconcerted by his expression. He looked stressed and upset. There was no time to speak to him. There were the confused sounds of people moving about, scraping chairs and voices which quietened down for the Deputy Head (he was still in post, Jim thought!) spoke briefly. He was welcoming the new Headmaster as well as the former pupils. His speech was also blessedly short, but no sooner had he thanked everyone, than a noisy band struck up. Conversation was impossible as guests decided to dance. Gemma decided the best thing to do was to follow suit. Jim was obviously not keen. To her surprise Gemma felt a tap on her shoulder and a tall, grinning woman, said "Excuse me. "Before either of them could ignore the interruption, Jim was whirled off into the throng. Gemma headed for the bar where, a few minutes later, Jim joined her. His expression was that of someone who has unexpectedly bitten into a Seville orange. Gemma handed him a glass of wine, took him firmly by the hand, and led him out of the hubbub into a corridor which served several classrooms. Thet were unlocked. She led him into the first one and sat down at one of the tables.

"Right," she said, looking him in the face, "what's all this about?"

Jim did not meet her gaze. He took a sip of his drink.

"What do you mean?" he asked.

Jim, you know what I mean. Ever since we came here you have been looking as though you're regretting it. Your Mr Jenkins is the only person that seems to be someone you like meeting."

He looked at her then. This time she could not understand his expression. She saw he was distressed. He looked away quickly. She waited.

"It's this place, "he said at last.

"But you've never been here before. This is a new building."

"I don't mean the school," he said, "It's Fallowfield, the entire town."

"Why on earth...?"

"Too many memories." He was struggling to explain. "I've never said much about my time here. It was not exactly pleasant."

"I see."

"No, you don't. How can you?" He paused for a while. "Life here was miserable," he said at last.

"But you can't have been all that unhappy at school," Gemma said, frowning as she tried to understand. "You did very well academically. I don't understand how you did so well if you were basically unhappy."

"Well, that's how it was."

"What about friends at school?" Gemma persisted. "You have never talked any school friends. Were you bullied or something?"

"Not exactly bullied. You realise my father was Deputy Head?"

"I thought that was your Mr Jenkins."

"Jenkins took over when we moved. He was my Maths teacher."

"Go on."

"What do you want to know?"

"Why you were unhappy."

"It's difficult when your father is Deputy Head, especially when he's in charge of discipline."

"Was it that bad?"

"It wasn't very good. You didn't know either of them, did you?"

"You know I didn't."

"They hated one another."

Gemma was shocked. She stared at him in disbelief. "You can't mean that," she said.

Jim did not reply. He was staring at the classroom wall and his expression was fixed in a rigid look in which Gemma read despair and intense regret. She got up and knelt by his chair an put her arms round him. But Jim did not respond. His body remained rigid. It was as though he was gripped by cramp. After a matter of minutes her knees began to hurt and awkwardly, she got to her feet. Jim came to life and stood up as well. Gemma reached up and kissed him on the cheek. He smiled uncertainly. "Sorry," he said.

"Do you want to go back to the hotel?" she asked.

"No, "he said. "I'll stretch my legs outside for a bit."

"OK. We can go back to the entrance. It's this way, I imagine."

"No. You go back to the party. I would like to be on my own for a little while. You go back and enjoy yourself. I'll come and find you."

"Are you sure?"

"Yes."

In the noisy hall Gemma took another glass of wine and was aware that this was her third glass. She found a seat and ignored the noise and the movement, trying to gather her thoughts. If Jim had told her about his unhappy growing up, she would never have insisted on attending this reunion. She drained her glass and collected another.

Jim shook her gently by the shoulder. She had fallen asleep. It was his turn to look concerned. He helped her to her feet and they wound an unsteady way to the entrance where Jim asked one of the helpers where he could phone for a taxi. His wife was unwell, he explained. The young man was concerned, used his own mobile phone to call a taxi, and assured Jim he would let Mr Morissoni know. Twenty minutes later they were back in their hotel room.

Jim woke up and turned over. Gemma was already dressed and searching in her handbag. She found a packet of paracetamol and swallowed two of them with a glass of water, then stepped out onto the little balcony. It was Sunday, Jim remembered. The road was silent. From the beach beyond the road came the soothing swish of small waves. He got out of bed and said good morning.

Gemma grimaced. "A hang-over," she said with disgust. "Now you're awake, I'll go downstairs while they're still serving breakfast. I'm desperate for coffee. If you get a move on, you might be in time. See you down there."

Breakfast was available one hour later Sundays, Jim remembered, and he hurried to find Gemma, nursing a large cup of hot coffee. He made himself some tea and joined her.

A familiar and faintly unctuous voice asked loudly, "How are you this morning? Better, I hope. I'm so sorry you had to leave early. You can relax for the day, however. It's going to be a beautiful day they say. "

Jim frowned, irritated by the intrusion.

"I'm fine this morning," Gemma lied. "It was probably all the noise that made me feel faint."

"A shame," said Joe. "It was a really splendid evening. Have a pleasant day and enjoy our little town."

"Ughj!" said Gemma as he walked away, bestowing his artificial smile on other guests.

Jim grinned conspiratorially. "At least we're only being charged half price," he said. "What do you want to do, leave early, drive home? I must say I don't much fancy driving."

"No," said Emma. "If you can bear it, I'd quite like to stay on for a couple of days."

Jim was clearly surprised. "Oh," he said, "I thought you would want to get away from the place as soon as you could. I'm sorry I spoiled the evening last night."

"I wish you had told me about your childhood before. I think it would be good for you to stay, face up to your past, so to speak. I'm sure there's nothing wrong with Fallowfield."

Jim looked at her thoughtfully. "If you want to stay," he said, "I'll stay, but I don't think a day or two here will sort out my problems. It's more complicated than that. I should have had all this out with my father before he died."

"Would you mind," Gemma asked, "if we found somewhere else to stay after tonight? I find Joe and his precious hotel – well, pretentious."

Jim laughed briefly. He agreed.

They found a spot on the beach. For a while they enjoyed watching the regular breaking of the small waves as the tide came in, but soon the sand was occupied by family parties and the quiet was replaced by the sound of children shouting. A group of teenagers began a game of cricket. The shoreline was busy with swimmers. Jim and Gemma brushed the sand from their clothes and headed for the coastal path. Neither spoke much, though both were deep in thought. Soon the shouts and screams were left behind. The beach gave way to small cliffs. Now the sound of the sea was continuous. At the top of a low rise, they paused and sat down again.

"I'm thirsty," Gemma declared. To her surprise Jim took a small bottle from his trouser pocket. "Breakfast!" he said. "It's a bit warm, but we can share it."

Again, they sat side by side, knees raised, arms round the.

"Don't ask me to talk about my childhood, not at the moment, anyhow. Can we forget the past for the moment? I've been trying to forget it for years. When we first met, my life started properly."

Gemma looked at him sharply. "OK," she said. She leaned over and kissed him. That was fine, she thought, but if her husband had kept the secret of his childhood from her ten years, were there other secrets? Sooner or later, she needed to know. Maybe this was not the time.

"About half a mile further," said Jim, "there's a small cove. You never know, they might sell drinks."

The path took a sudden little dive into a rocky inlet where four small boats lay on a rocky shelf. There was no one to be seen but a board, pinned to the wall of one of the cottages advertised drinks and ice creams. They bought both before resuming their walk, turning inland along a wide bridle path. They did not talk, taking in the sights and smells of the countryside. At last, they arrived back at the outskirts of the town. It was early afternoon.

"I imagine we have missed lunch," Jim said.

He was right, but the helpful girl on the reception desk suggested they try room service. She also reached behind her and talk an envelope from a pigeonhole. It was addressed to Jim who took it with him as they returned to their room. They sat on the balcony and ate soup.

The note was from Mr Jenkins, a reminder that he would like to talk to Jim. He realised that they had left the reunion ball early and, in the circumstances, he thought they might leave Fallowfield earlier than planned. He would be in all day on Sunday, he said, if Jim could find an hour to visit him. Just turn up, he wrote.

"You go then," Gemma said. "It's not as though we have planned anything. I'll wander down to the beach again until it gets too hot. If it does, I'll head for the nearest café or come back to the hotel. Go on chat to your old friend."

Jim was not entirely sure that he wanted to spend an hour with Mr Jenkins. It would be another are of reminiscing and the old man would be clearly interested in finding out how Jim had spent the 25 years since he and his family had left the town. He remembered the leaving because it had seemed hurried. There was little explanation, simply a very great sense of urgency about the move. His parents, as always, had squabbled throughout the operation. Jim had tried to keep out of the way, only to be accused of shirking. He remembered only hoping that life in the new town would be somehow an improvement, though he had not seen how it might be. It had not been much of an improvement at all. However, he had been able to sign up to a course at the local college which would eventually lead to a qualification. He had hoped to continue with mathematics, Kane her degree, possibly try to follow a career as an academic. Mathematics was his true love. Instead, he had accepted as second best for much more restricted training.

Mr Jenkins was very grateful that Jim had come to see him. He had watched his pupil grow into early manhood. He liked the boy and saw in him the potential to do extremely well, but he had, like everybody else in Fallowfield, it seemed, completely lost touch of him. He was now eager to discover if his hopes for his former pupil had come to fruition.

"I often wondered what had become of you," he said, as the two men sat in the comfortable conservatory. "Did you make it to university?"

Jim stared out across the lawn, trying not to reveal the disappointment he still felt after ¼ of a century

. "No," he said. "Things did not work out as planned. I don't know how much you remember or knew about me and my father."

"Well, don't forget he was then the Deputy Head. In some ways he was my boss. I'm afraid I did not get on with him but, to tell the truth, not many people did. How is he by the way?"

Jim took a deep breath. This was exactly the kind of conversation he would prefer to avoid. "You will probably realise why he left so suddenly. There was some kind of scandal involving one of the girls."

Mr Jenkins nodded. "Yes, I'm afraid I learned all about it. The whole business was very badly handled. My own part in the affair was far from blameless, too, but I have tried to excuse myself because I will still a young man, an experience. I went along with my elders and, as I thought then, my betters. Everyone, including the then headmaster and the governors were terrified of scandal and thought they could avoid it. I believe the girl in question was paid off, a bit like your father. It was, of course, doubly disgraceful that they backed his application for another job in teaching. But this possibly very painful for you."

"It is," said Jim. "It killed my father in the end."

Mr Jenkins turned in his chair, clearly shocked by this statement. "Killed him, you say?"

"He took his own life two years later," Jim explained. "Drove his car into a brick wall, part of the bridge."

"My dear fellow, I'm so sorry!"

Jim said nothing for a long time. His mind was like a cinema screen on which meaningless signs and symbols chased one another. He felt only bitterness. After a very long time he pulled himself together, set up in the chair and said, "I should never have come back. It was Gemma, my wife, who thought it would be a good idea." He raised his eyes as though uncomprehending. "She of course had no idea about any of this. Both my parents were dead when I married Gemma. She gave me a new start. We've had 20 years of good, happy marriage. Coming back to Fallowfield has brought it all back, like digging up a corpse – two corpses – my mother lasted two years, most of it in a mental hospital, then she died too."

"Jim, I simply don't know what to say. You have had a dreadful time."

"I thought it was all forgotten!" Jim cried in pain. "I should have known better. It seems the past has a way of catching up on you."

"I imagine your dreams of University collapsed?"

"Oh yes, no chance," Jim's bitterness was now obvious.

"Look," Mr Jenkins said, "nothing I can say can possibly help you. But in all this you weren't to blame. You were innocent. I doubt if anybody even explain to you what was going on."

"No, you are right. It was only after they were both dead that I learned about this. I discovered that my father, man I didn't like, in fact, I hated him most of the time, he was a swaggering bully – my mother should have left him years before this – but here he was, a man who was supposed to set an example for his pupils, abusing them, at least one of them. I learned of all this only when he died. I have no idea who the girl was."

"I imagine everybody breathed a sigh of relief when he left. As for the girl, I think she moved to Colchester. I knew her, of course. A sweet little thing, she wasn't even 16 at the time. The most disgraceful thing was the way in which it was all hushed up. The governors paid her to keep her mouth shut and she did, as far as I know. I was too busy trying to come to terms with my new job. Of course, I felt guilty and that guilt has never quite gone away. What a sad world we live in!" Both men sat for a while, preoccupied with sad thoughts. After a while Mr Jenkins stood up and went into the house.

He came back with a tray and set about pouring tea for both.

"Well, "he said, and sent to sound more cheerful, "maybe it's time we both put the past behind us. We can't change it. I shall always have to live with the guilt, but there is no need for you to feel it. You have done nothing wrong. I am very, very sorry I brought all this up back to you."

"It was coming back to this place," said Jim, "not you. I had completely pushed all these memories way back in my mind. Then Joe contacted me about the proposed reunion. I didn't want to come. Perhaps, if Gemma hadn't seen the invitation ..."

"Too many ifs and buts, my son. The past has happened. The moving finger writes, and having writ. You must look away. You can't wipe it clean like a blackboard."

"Do they still use chank? "Jim asked. "I thought all the blackboards were whiteboards these days."

The old man acknowledged the attempt at humour with a mild laugh. "That's better," he said "You can't forget all this stuff, but you can't let it ruin the rest of your life."

"I hope not," Jim said, suddenly more positive. "I just wish I had told Gemma about all this years ago. I think it has come as a real shock."

"Well, I hope you sorted out," said Mr Jenkins. He took a sip of his tea. "You say you had 20 good years with Gemma?"

"Yes, we have had a really good time together."

"So, you never made it to university. What have you been doing. What a shame to waste all that mathematical ability."

"I am an accountant," Jim sounded rueful.

"Lots of arithmetic, not exactly exciting?"

"It has its compensations. It pays quite well. I'm self-employed. We can take oddities when we feel like it and we done a lot of travelling. And I like my clients. It has not been too bad, I suppose."

"There you are then stop it sounds so your life has been quite successful."

"I suppose so."

"What about your wife? That she has a job?"

"She's a solicitor. A bit like me. She finds the job less than demanding, but she enjoys the freedom. We don't have any children." He added the last sentence as an afterthought.

He found his wife here the beach. She had walked as far as the wharf to look at the two ships. They were identical, she said, but the boards on which their trips were announced suggested they tended to go in opposite directions. Maybe it was something they could do the next day. How had the visit to Mr Jenkins gone? It had been interesting, Jim said, but he did not elaborate. It had done him good, he realised. He would try to take the old man's advice, turned his back firmly on the past, learn to enjoy the present as, indeed, he had been enjoying it before the invitation to the reunion had popped up on his laptop.

They enjoyed their last meal at Joe's hotel, secretly glad they would move to somewhere more modest in the morning. It had been a pleasant day which Gemma had found very relaxing. Jim's meeting with his old teacher had once more brought up memories he had tried to suppress. The repeated assurance that he was not to blame for any of the misery and unhappiness of his childhood and adolescence, an assurance which no one else had given him, felt like an absolution, as though his sins had been forgiven or rather he had been told he had not sinned at all.

He slipped into the luxurious bed next to his wife. She smelled appetisingly fragrant. He ran his hand over the curve of her hip and into the smooth valley of her waist. Gemma caught his hand with hers and rejected it firmly, pushing it away and muttering, "No, Jim. I need time." Hurt, he turned away and lay on his back. He lay like this for a long time. Outside, an occasional vehicle swished along the road. There was no wind. The gentle, rhythmic sound of the sea was soothing. His head was busy with confused and conflicting ideas. He slowly tried to accept Gemma's rejection, though surely, he was the victim, wasn't he? The reassurance of the talk with the old teacher was replaced by a form of anxiety. Gemma's breathing slowed as she fell asleep. He could not relax but did not want to wake her by getting out of bed. He wished again that he had never shown the email to Gemma, but had let sleeping dogs lie. That would not have worked, however. The guilt which had hung about for years would have surfaced sooner or later. It had perhaps ben purged today, but the effect of the revelation on Gemma was something he was not prepared for.

Unable to remain there at last, he slipped out of bed and made a cup of tea which he took out to the balcony. It was two o'clock. He went back to bed waking Gemma.

"You're cold!" she protested, then fell asleep again. This time Jim fell asleep as well.

Chapter Two

The road was noticeably noisier when they woke. Of course, Jim told himself as he waited for Gemma to emerge from the shower, it was Monday, a working day. Gemma was her bright, breezy self, but he was sluggish from lack of sleep. They said little but ate breakfast in the restaurant which seemed full of weary people who thought only of leaving quickly. Jim and Gemma followed suit. Jim settled the bill, frowning at the price of extras, including the use of wi-fi. Joe, helping on the reception desk, wished them a good journey but was unable to be as effusive as he might have been. He said what a shame it had been that Gemma had been ill and so obliged to miss much of the reunion. Then they retrieved the car. Gemma drove.

They found a cluster of B and B signs in one of the older, residential streets on the other, inland side of the town. They picked one at random, a 1930s semi. They parked on the tarmac drive and rang the bell. She was busy with her chores, she explained. She had barely finished tiding the room in question but, provided they were not too concerned about the rest of the house, they were welcome to inspect the bedroom. She was young, thought Gemma, probably in her twenties. She wore a wedding ring. Her name was Jean Carter.

The room was clean with an en suite bathroom and cost less than half the reduced rate in the Morissoni Hotel. It was available for the rest of the week. Jim accepted on the spot.

"I hope you don't mind bringing your own bags upstairs," she said. "My husband will fetch them for you later, if you can wait."

"It's OK," said Jim. "I'll do that. We've only got a couple of cases. Would you prefer us to come back later?"

"O, Lord no. I'm sorry I'm still in my morning muddle."

"What does your husband do?" Gemma asked.

"He's an electrician. We've only had this place six months and he's busy bringing it up to date. So far he has rewired everything. You may have noticed he has fitted a decent shower in your room."

"Sounds like a very handy man to have around."

"Yes, he is. He reckons it will take about two years to complete the plumbing, and then he'll start on what he calls the big stuff. The trouble is, he has to fit everything round his work."

"He works for someone else, does he?" Jim asked.

"For the time being," she said. "He's built himself a workshop in the garden."

Before they had time to end the conversation, she ushered them through a kitchen into a slightly run-down garden to point out the wooden workshop.

"I'd better fetch those cases," Jim said.

"Oh, I'm sorry. I shouldn't be keeping you talking," the young woman said.

"That's all right," Jim said. "Can I ask, do you have wi-fi?"

She had, she said. "I'll have to find the password. It's usually on the router."

"Oh yes. I'll show you. It's in the sitting room. "

"Thank you," Jim said. "If you don't mind, I'll log on before we gout again."

"Of course. You'll be wanting to let people at home know you've arrived."

"No, indeed to speak to a couple of clients to rearrange our appointments."

"Clients?"

"I'm an accountant."

"Oh, I see." She probably did not see, thought Gemma, left temporarily to her own devices in the hallway. Jim returned with the larger of the two cases. Jean was carrying the other and the laptop. She led the way to the bedroom, came back down to help Jim locate the router, then turned, flustered, to Gemma.

"Don't worry about my husband," Gemma said, secretly amused that their early arrival should have caused such uproar. "If you give me the Visitors' Book, I'll fill it in for you while we wait. I don't want to hold you up any longer."

Jean watched unashamedly as Gemma took the ornate book and signed in. "Oh, you have come quite a long way!" Jean commented. "I never thought. You must be tired. I haven't even offered you a cup of tea."

Gemma explained they had merely moved from the Morissoni Hotel, which provoked more comments.

"Grainer," she read. "I'm sure I've heard the name before. Do you have relations here?"

"No," said Gemma, as her husband reappeared. "Look, we'll get out of your way now. We'll be back later this afternoon."

"Oh, right," Jean said. "I'll give you a key."

Jim drove back into the town centre. He was still tired. They did a little window shopping before drinking coffee in a smart bar.

"Young Mrs Carter," Gemma said, said she had heard the name Grainger recently. I forgot to droves tell her I met a Mrs Carter on Saturday. I wonder if they are related."

"Could be, I suppose. It's a small town."

They sat for a while in a small, well-kept park at the top of n a hill. Frem here they had a good view of the town and the bay. The waterfront was busy in contrast to the weekend. Jim pointed out buildings he remembered and led her to what had once been his school. It had been converted into a block of flats at one end of the street. But much of the original building and what had been playing field was now a group of houses.

"It's funny," Jim said, "but I don't much care about the changes. I was never especially happy here. Mind you, I don't much like the new buildings either."

He had expected to be somehow upset, affected by memories, but he wasn't. Fallowfield was virtually an unknown town.

They bought tickets for a trip on the Mermaid for the two o'clock sailing and ate lunch in a small pub first. The landlord was serving at the bar. He was a middle-aged man who seemed to be staring at Jim. Eventually, he came over to their table.

"Excuse me," he said, "but aren't you the couple who came to the reunion and left early?"

Jimm admitted it.

"I only ask because your wife was ill." He looked at Gemma. "I hope you're OK now."

"Yes, thank you. I'm fine, enjoying your wonderful fish."

The barman laughed. "Caught last night," he said. "I'm glad you like it, and I'm glad you've recovered. I'm sorry, but I didn't catch your name."

"Grainger," said Jim, and a brief, involuntary expression of shock crossed the man's face before he smiled once more.

"Bon appetite!" he said and went back to the bat. Jim looked at his wife and raised his eyebrows quizzically, but Gemma said nothing and turned her attention once more to her food. Jim paid the bill and they headed for the wharf. The short encounter left Jim mildly uneasy.

The trip in the tangy, salty air was refreshing and enjoyable. Over the tannoy system a commentator supplied information about the shoreline and wildlife. There was a surprising variety of birds, especially when the ship circumnavigated a small, rocky island.

"Wish we had binoculars," said Jim. He took many pictures which Gemma suggested would turn out ninety percent sea, but he might, he said, be able to select and enlarge bits of them later. Gemma was pleased to see his happily distracted. The trip, she thought, would probably be the highlight of their visit to Fallowfield.

The following morning over breakfast Jim said that he wanted to go back into town and browse in the bookshops. He wanted to find a decent guide to birdwatching, he said. Gemma wish him well but said she would find her own way into town later.

"I lost two fingernails yesterday," she explained, holding out her hand. Jim was alarmed until he realised, she meant two artificial nails.

"Don't go right into town," Jean advised. "Crossover the road as far as Maple Street. There's a small flight of shops there and one of them is a hairdressers. I think it's called Head to Toe. Anyway, her charges are quite reasonable. She might not be too busy. She's only been there a few months."

So, Gemma found her way to Maple Street while Jim walked into the centre of the little town to find a decent bookshop. The owner of the shop, a young woman called Sophie, was busy with a customer. She stopped briefly to talk to Gemma, who held out her hand to show the missing nails.

"Oh dear," Sophie said. "I see your problem. I am afraid I can't simply match the other nails. I would have to do a complete manicure."

"Is there any way you can fit me in? I don't live here, you see, I'm just visiting."

"As it happens," said Sophie, "I'm free once I've finished with Mrs Hutchings." She gestured towards the lady in the chair. Gemma was delighted. Sophie gave her a bowl of warm water in which to soak her fingers while she waited. Sophie returned to

Mrs Hutchings to put the final touches to her hair. Gemma was sitting at a small table in front of a very large mirror. She could see the door clearly and anybody passing by. Suddenly a young man opened the door and stepped inside. He was waving his phone excitedly. His voice was strangely familiar as he called, "Mum! I've got it!"

Sophie turned away from Mrs Hutchings. "Damien! Calm down. Got what?"

"A junior lectureship!" He was still extremely excited. "I told you about it. This is my big chance, the first step on the ladder."

"Congratulations!" Sophie said. It was obvious that she was not sure what her son meant. The young man wrapped his arms around his mother, lifted her off her feet, and weld her briefly in the confined space.

"Damien, this is not really the place," Sophie said.

"Sorry," said the young man. "I just had to tell somebody. Sorry, ladies," he gave his mother a resounding case on the forehead – she was several inches shorter than him – then, without more ado, he left has quickly as he had arrived. Mrs Hutchings was laughing.

"I am so sorry," Sophie apologised. "It's my son, Damien. I think he was telling me he'd landed a job at the University. I think it's a lecturer's job – mathematics."

But Gemma was still staring at the mirror. She was transfixed. For a few, brief seconds she thought the intruder was Jim. His voice was very similar, but it was his face which confused her. She could have sworn it was Jim, perhaps a slightly younger version, a bewildering copy of the young man who had greeted her as she walked down the aisle all those years ago. She sat, her fingers still in the warm water, and began to recover her senses. She was still in a state of shock when the hairdresser took payment from Mrs Hutchings and turned her attention to Gemma.

"Are you all right?" Sophie asked, "you look a bit pale."

"I'm all right, but could I have a glass of water?"

Sophie waited until she had taken a drink then took her left hand and began removing the artificial nails.

"I hope it wasn't Damien," she said. "He knows better than disturbing at work, but he is obviously very excited about this job."

"Well, so it should be. It sounds like the chance of a lifetime."

Sophie was smiling with pride. "I don't understand any of the things he deals with," she said. "I was never any good at all and maths."

"How old is your son? He's not exactly a teenager, is he? You look far too young to be his mother."

"I was very young," Sophie admitted.

Gemma's growing suspicions were confirmed. She said nothing more as the manicurist continued with her work. Her mind was very busy. She was trying to work out dates stop she asked Sophie how old her son was.

"Damien? He's 23. Why do you ask?"

"I'm sorry," Gemma said, "you must think I'm very nosy."

"I told you, I was very young when I had him."

A frightening was forming in Gemma's mind was Damien Jim's son? Was this another secret? Perhaps – and this was even more difficult – Jim had been sowing his wild oats even at the age of 18, and this was the result which he did not even know about. Whatever the truth of the matter, she would like to get to the bottom of it. How could she discover the truth without causing a great deal of pain?

"That will be thirty pounds" Sophie said, when Gemma declared herself more than satisfied with her new nails. Gemma found her purse and took out her card to pay. Sophie glanced at it before touching the card reader and froze for a moment before taking the payment.

"Grainger," she exclaimed.

At that moment an elderly lady with blue hair came in.

"I think we need to talk," Gemma said.

"Yes, I'd say we do!" Sophie looked angry. She closed at 5.39, she said hurriedly. Could Gemma come back then? Gemma agreed. She left the salon and walked into town as far as the park where she and Jim had been. She sat on the same seat and tried to work it out. Once more she was seriously challenging the decision they had made to come to the Reunion.. She and Jim had been happy, almost perfectly happy, before they had returned to Fallowfield. It occurred to her that she did not really know if Jim had been successful in suppressing memories of his past, but the subject had never come up before. He had not seen too upset when they first arrived. Indeed, the sight of his old school, or what was left of it, had not provoked too many memories. His chat with his former teacher seemed also to have settled his mind nicely. Curiously enough she, Gemma, was the one who had been more ill at ease than her husband. She was very well aware that she pushed him away in bed, that she did not physically want him at the moment, and she was at something of a loss to explain why.

The encounter with Sophie and her son had come as a shock. Damien looks extraordinarily life Jim. It could not be coincidence. The obvious explanation was that Sophie, who had admitted that she was very young at the time, has had a teenage affair with young Jim. It was perfectly possible that Jim had forgotten all about it but surely he should be told he had a son, if that were indeed the case? In the meantime, she could say nothing to her husband without more information, information that could only come from Sophie. That might prove quite difficult. If guess was correct, Sophie had brought up her son as a single mother. That must have been difficult. If it was the case, Jim would be very badly shaken by the news, but both he and Sophie needed to be brought up to date. So, for that matter, did Damien, who deserved to know the truth about his parentage. And where did this leave her, Gemma? She seemed to have acquired a stepson.

Her phone rang. It was Jim.

"I've been to a great bookshop. It belongs to a chap called Jay. He happens to be a keen birdwatcher and when I told him I was just starting, he was helpful. Better than that, he's planning to take his boat out to the island this afternoon and he's invited me to go with him."

"What sort of boat?"

Jim laughed. "Quite substantial, judging by the pictures. Anyway, I'm ringing to ask if it's OK with you."

"I don't fancy another trip."

"No, I meant would you mind if I go with him and leave you to find something to amuse yourself."

"No, you go ahead. I've got things to do."

"Oh, good."

Gemma was relieved. She had to kill time until half past five, when she would talk to Sophie in an attempt to uncover the truth. Sophie's reaction to the name Grainger was worrying. Meanwhile, Gemma took a bus to one of the nearby villages, wandered along country lanes, talking to friendly horses and curious cows, and returned to the town in time to have tea in one of the cafes. At five thirty promptly she met Sophie as she locked up. There was an all-day pub nearby which Sophie might be a good place to talk. "I've been on my feet all day," she said so I want somewhere to sit down."

The pub served tea, so they found a quiet table and sat down.

"The name Grainger isn't all that common," Sophie said. "That's why I reckon it's no coincidence you're here."

Gemma nodded. "It must look suspicious," she said, "but I promise you we didn't come here to, well, to spy on you. I don't know what your connection with the Grainger family is, but I must tell you, your son – well, he's the spitting image of my husband when he was younger."

"Your husband?"

"Jim."

Sophie looked puzzled. "I don't understand," she said.

"Forgive the personal questions. I just wondered if, maybe, you and Jim were at school together. He left Fallowfield when he was eighteen."

"When was that?"

"Twenty-five years ago."

Sophie frowned. "Damien is 23. Your husband was eighteen, you say. He is certainly not Damien's father."

"I'm very sorry. The similarity."

Sophie was silent for a long time. "All right," she said at last. "I was going to say this is none of your business, but perhaps it is. You may find this hard to understand, but when I was fifteen years old, I fell in love with an older man. He was my teacher and his name was Grainger."

"Your teacher?"

"Yes. Of course, people found out and there was a dreadful fuss. Jack – that was his name – was sacked."

"At the name, Jack, Gemma flinched. Things began to fall into place. "And he left you pregnant?" she asked in horror.

"He didn't know, nor did I at the time. I really thought I loved him and I was heart-broken when the school governors..."

"The school knew?" Gemma was astonished.

"I think they must have been terrified of the scandal. They didn't want any talk. They sent Jack away. There was Jack himself and his wife and..."

"And Jim." Gemma finished the sentence.

"That's right. They made me sign something, a document of non-disclosure, I think they call it. They gave my Dad a lot of money to move away. That's why I've only just move to Fallowfield."

"And it was only then that you found you were pregnant."

Sophie nodded. "I fought to keep him," she said.

"You were fifteen?"

"Sixteen."

Gemma did some quick mental arithmetic. "That means you must be forty-one, and Damien is twenty-five."

Sophie nodded. "I never knew what became of Jack," she said. "He must be well into his sixties by now. As time went by, my opinion about him changed. He was my teacher, after all. I suppose what he did was a betrayal of trust."

"Jack died two years after all this."

"Died?"

Gemma did not explain further.

"Well I never! I sometimes felt sorry for his wife, not that I knew her."

"She died soon after Jack."

Gemma called for fresh tea. The revelations had created a bond between the two women. They sat in thought for a while.

"What next?" asked Gemma.

"Next?"

"If I've got this right, Jim and Damien are half-brothers."

"Oh, so they are!"

"Do we tell them, or should we keep this a secret between us?

"I don't know." Sophie gave a curious giggle.

"What's funny?"

"We are half-sisters-in-law."

"I suppose that's true."

"I don't know how you feel, but I want a bit more time to think about it."

"I think I do, too. Though there seem to have been a lot of secrets so far."

They left it at that, but agreed to meet again before the end of the week, since Gemma did not know how much longer she and Jim would stay in Fallowfield.

Any fears Jim might suspect she was hiding something were soon ended when they met for dinner in a decent restaurant before returning to their lodgings. He was eager to report on his day with Jay. Gemma was amused by his almost child-like enthusiasm He opened his expensive Guide to Seabirds, then he waxed lyrical over opened the Guide to Garden Birds. In a separate sketchbook he had made recognisable drawings of birds he had seen. In another book there were illustrations of garden and inland birds which he would look out for. He gave no more than a glance at Gemma's new nails.

Fresh air, a new interest and healthy food brought him back to life. The holiday seemed to be doing him a great deal of good. Only Jean showed any interest in Gemma's manicure. She made everyone a drink of cocoa as they made their way to bed. Jim made no demands on his wife, being obviously tired. Gemma was pleased. She was pleased to see him happy, but her feelings were little more than friendly and companionable. She wondered how he would react to the startling news that he had a half-brother. She was also curious to discover what Damien was like. It was remarkable that he was also apparently gifted as a mathematician. And with these thoughts she fell asleep.

"You're supposed to be on holiday," Gemma protested as her husband took the laptop back to the bedroom.

"I know, but it's Mr Worthing. He is in a muddle and quite anxious about his tax liabilities. I just want to reassure him that he hasn't done anything wrong and he won't finish up in jail. He is a nice chap, just doesn't really understand money."

"All right, "Gemma was resigned. "But we haven't decided what we want to do with the day. Any ideas?"

"I have. Jay..."

"Jay?"

"The man in the bookshop."

"Oh, that Jay. You seem to be getting very friendly."

"Yes, it's a shared interest."

"Birdwatching?"

"Yes, he really got me interested."

"So, don't tell me you're going to spend the day with Jay?"

"No. He did point out there is a wildlife sanctuary place about 30 miles away. He suggested we might like to visit it."

"You and Jay?"

"No, me and you. Apparently it has a proper visitor centre with a café. I thought you might like to come with me."

"Well, it's not beach weather," Gemma commented, "and I don't have any other ideas. Where is this place?"

Jim opened his phone and found a local map. The Wetlands Bird Centre was easy to locate. Gemma agreed to go with him to the Centre once he had made his call to Bill Worthing. She took advantage of his absence to phone Sophie. She explained she would be away all day and asked if her half-sisters-in-law had come to any decision about telling her son that he had a brother. No, Sophie told her, she was still thinking about it and his possible reaction. It was also on her mind that she did not know Jim.

"I've been thinking about how Jim will take it, too," Gemma admitted.

"It could be a disaster."

"I agree, but I don't think we have the right not to tell them."

There was a brief silence, then Sophie said, "I just hope we get this right. I've got to go, sorry, my first customer has arrived."

Jim was cheerful as they drove to the wildlife centre. He understood it was going to be a pleasant place for the general visitor. You did not need to be an enthusiast or expert, he said.

"As long as it has a good café," said Gemma.

"I may push the boat out," Jim warned her, "and buy a pair of binoculars."

"It's your money. You've earned it." For many years they had agreed a system whereby their personal earnings remain largely separate. They shared domestic expenses like the mortgage and food, keeping the rest in their own, personal accounts. It worked well. When it came to sudden, large expenditure, such as booking holidays or buying large items for the house, they would consult, otherwise they each had plenty of pocket money. Gemma was a little curious that Jim should mention his proposed purchase of a pair of binoculars all the same. She wondered how much they were likely to cost.

They arrived, parked, bought tickets and walked in. There was a well-stocked shop at the entrance. Beyond, glass doors led to the first of a series of ponds. The surface of the pond was busy with waterfowl of differing sizes, including a pair of swans and a whole flotilla of ducks. But before venturing further, Jim was already looking at a display of equipment which included binoculars and telescopes. Gemma left him to it and browse amongst the books. Most of them were guides but there were also a number of titles which were clearly related to wildlife in general and Gemma looked through several of these. Jim had enlisted the help of an assistant, a young woman who seemed very knowledgeable. Gemma heard a few words, "objective", "ratio", "acuity". She was not interested, though she was seeing her husband in a new light. He seemed to show all the enthusiasm of a young boy. Gemma realised her feelings towards him at that moment were quite maternal. It came as a little shop.

Jim was waving a pair of binoculars in her direction, obviously wanting her approval. She walked over, said hello to the salesperson, and took the proffered item from Jim's hand.

"What do you think?" he asked eagerly.

"I haven't a clue," Gemma said, looking at the smart object in her hand.

"Penny here recommends them," Jim said. "They are quite expensive though."

Gemma looked at the ticket and suppressed a gasp. "It's your money," she said. "If you think you're going to use them..."

Jim made the purchase, then led the way through the glass doors to the first pond. From the small map she had picked up in the shop Gemma knew there were six of these. She saw a muddy pool of water, fringed at the far side by weedy plants. The surface of the pond was busy with scores of small ducks. Gemma could not identify more than one species, nor was she inclined to do so. Jim was already busy with his new purchase, adjusting the focus and making little appreciative noises. This, thought Gemma, was not a hobby for her. She followed Jim as he made his way to pond number two. This was a larger one and the management had sensibly provided benches. Next to the benches were painted display boards, indicating the various birds to be seen. There was also a large rubbish bin and a metal box containing clean newspapers, on which there was a printed notice in red. It advised visitors to take at least two sheets of the paper to protect their clothing and to dispose of them in the bin provided. One glance at the bench explained the warning. Gemma opened the box and retrieved several sheets of newspaper which she spread on the seat.

"You go ahead," she said. "I'm going to stay here for a while. No need to hurry."

No, this was not her choice of pastime. She was far from certain that the newspaper would be terribly effective. When Jim disappeared around a small hillock on his way to ponder number three, she stood up and gingerly examined the newspaper. It was, thankfully, still clean. Very carefully she bundled it up and stuffed it into the waste bin, then she headed back towards the entrance, the café and, most importantly, the washrooms. She sat with more tea and a bun and waited for Jim. She was content to view the birds on pond number one through the glass windows.

After a very long time Jim rejoined her. He was disappointed that she showed so little enthusiasm. He suggested they find somewhere to eat in the countryside, preferably with a garden. He would, he said, be perfectly happy to use his new binoculars watching other birds than ducks and geese. Gemma became the driver, suppressing her growing irritation as her husband opened the window on the passenger side and strove to identify objects at a distance as they drove past. The irritation continued when they found a pleasant pub and sat in an orchard at the back to eat a bland meal. I suppose, Gemma said to herself, this makes me a birdwatching widow. Jim, preoccupied, did not notice her irritation or frustration which continued until they arrived back in Fallowfield's.

Gemma had made her mind up. Having spent the day with Jim, who had treated her company with such indifference, she had grown mildly resentful. Why should she allow her husband's previously unknown past to cause her anxiety? After all, it had nothing much to do with her. She had, it's true, discovered an unknown brother-in-law in Damien, but his existence was something over which she had never had any control. As for her concern at Jim's possible reaction to learning of Damien's existence, well, that was for him to deal with. He was, after all, more than forty years old, old enough to deal with such shocks. As for Damien, he, too was a mature man of twenty-three or four. The concern she and Sophie shared was in the end unnecessary. The facts were facts and could not be changed or undone. She would speak to Sophie the next day and tell her how she felt.

Her mood was lifted a little when they discovered the cinema was showing a film they both wanted to see. They settled in the darkness. Jim had bought popcorn, although he knew Gemma disapproved and found the smell offensive. She thought he wanted to feed wheat to the geese and swans and he was eating revolting popcorn himself. She was thankful when it was finished, but she wondered if he would have any appetite for a meal afterwards. He had. Gemma reflected with amusement that the day in general illustrated what people meant when talked of a marriage having lost its shine.

In the morning once more Gemma phoned Sophie while Jim turned his attention to his clients. She agreed to meet the hairdresser at lunchtime. Gemma told Jim she needed to return to the hairdressers because there was a problem with one of the nails. Jim was happy to find his way down to the waterfront. With his new glasses and books he was now equipped. He might also call in at the bookshop to show Jay his purchase and seeks his approval.

Gemma told Sophie of her decision. Sophie was still a little uncertain but she agreed that her son was not a child any longer and deserved to be told the truth. It was not, she commented, like telling a child he was adopted. She had not deliberately been keeping the information to herself until the past two days. Her only question was when and how the two men should be told of their relationship. This was something that Gemma had not fully thought through. Perhaps the best solution, she suggested, would be to get them together and tell them both at the same time. They discussed the mechanics of this operation. The time was against them because Jim and Genna intended to drive home on Saturday. The only problem would be if Damien was not free. A quick call from his mother confirmed that he had no plans for that evening and that he would happily meet her for dinner. She told him nothing more except to say that she wanted him to meet two people, visitors to the town that she thought he would find interesting. She explained that they were going home on Saturday.

They met in one of the pubs which Jim and Genna had discovered. It served excellent food and was generally quiet. That evening the small dining room was empty. Gemma had told her husband she wanted him to meet a new friend, the young woman who had dealt with her nails. Jim thought it a strange friendship, but said yes. The stage was set.

Jim and Gemma arrived first and took the seats at the far end of the small room and ordered drinks. Ten minutes later Sophie and her son arrived. Sophie made her way towards the table.

"Oh, here she is!" said Gemma. She sounded oddly nervous. Jim was looking at Sophie, surprised that she was a little younger than Gemma had given him to believe. When her son appeared behind her, Jim shifted his attention. The light in the dining room was quite low, and he merely noticed a well-built young man. A waitress came over to take their orders for drinks. There was a slightly awkward silence

"Congratulations!" Gemma said, looking at Damien.

Damien, confused, looked from Gemma to his mother. "Congratulations? I do not understand." Then, "Oh, you must have been in the salon when I burst in. So sorry."

"You're right," Gemma said, "but that's not why we're here."

Damien looked more puzzled than ever, his gaze moving from one woman to the other.

"Can someone tell me what's going on?" Jim intervened.

"Yes, this affects both of you," Gemma said.

"What are we not congratulating someone for?"

"When Sophie here was about to do my nails," Gemma explained, "Damien came in briefly to tell her he had been offered a new post at the University."

"I see," said Jim. "Then congratulations are certainly in order. Well done, young man! What kind of post?"

"Junior lecturer in mathematics," Damien said, clearly trying to remain modest while bursting with pride.

"Mathematics! That's really something," said Jim, but his expression was not one of pleased appreciation, reflecting the young man's pride. Gemma was looking at him with curiosity and disapproval, not understanding and hoping that the other two did not see what she saw.

"So, if that's not it," Jim said, "why are we all here?"

No one answered immediately. Gemma and Sophie exchanged glances. The two men remained puzzled.

"Sophie and I were talking," Gemma said at last. She was speaking very slowly, as though counting each word like a miser with his coins. She had everyone's attention.

"It revolved around the name Grainger."

"What about it?" Jim was looking wary now.

"We discovered, Jim, that you and Damien have – a great deal in common."

"You're talking in riddles," said Jim. He sounded a little irritated.

"It's something I don't talk about much," Sophie said. She turned to Damien. "I've never told you anything much about your father, have I?"

Damien was looking very apprehensive. "No," he said. "Are you about to tell me...?"

"I am not your father!" Jim was now quite angry. He spoke emphatically, as though rebutting a false claim before it had been voiced.

"No," Gemma said, once more her voice was low as she tried to lower the emotional intensity. "You are not his father, you are his brother."

There was no reply to this. Both men looked horror- stricken as they tried to take in the information. They stared at one another.

"You even look alike," Gemma pointed out. "Surely you can see that."

On one wall of the pub there was a mirror, decorated with the brand name of beer sold. Damien got to his feet to go and stare at his image. After hesitating, Jim walked across the room to join him. The two men stared at their images together. There was an obvious age difference. Damien's skin was fresher, cleaner, younger. Fine lines around the eyes betrayed some of Jim's history. The shape of the mouth and especially of the eyes, however, held them both. They stood like this for some time then, without speaking, they walked back to their places. Both picked up their drinks and drained them as the waitress came back to take their orders.

"Refills all round," Jim said, his voice hoarse and slightly shaky. "And two double brandies." Neither Gemma nor Sophie said a word. From a nearby bar in another room came the sound of people laughing. Here there was only a profound silence, but a silence so full of emotion that no one dared speak for a long time. The waitress reappeared with a tray of drinks and for a few moments the silence was broken by the clinking of glasses. Still no one spoke until the young girl had left the room, then Jim lifted his double brandy, held it briefly as an ironic salute to his newly found brother, who matched his actions, then he took a large mouthful that took his breath for a moment.

"Explain!" He ordered in the same, strange, voice.

Gemma began. She explained that her long dead father-in-law, Jim's father, had been having an affair twenty-six years previously. "He was a senior teacher at the local school," Sophie explained. Her eyes were fixed on her son, as though pleading for forgiveness.

 "I never met him, as Jim will tell you, "Gemma added.so I knew nothing of this until I met Sophie."

"I was in love with him," Sophie said." I really loved him and I thought he loved me. I was fifteen."

Damien looked thoroughly shocked, not sure he could understand what he was being told. His mother told him how the couple had been forcibly separated and how Jack Grainger had been made to leave. "I never saw him again," she said.

"But he left you with me as a farewell present!" said Damien. It was not clear if he was furiously angry.

"Neither of us knew that I was pregnant." Sophie was very distressed, reaching out to her son. After a moment he responded, taking her in his arms awkwardly on the dining room chairs. Gemma, too, was in tears. Jim was silent but Gemma had never seen him so angry. He consoled himself by finishing the brandy.

The waitress reappeared, hoping this time to take their orders for food. She did not know what to do when she saw there was obviously something upsetting them all. She muttered something about coming back later and left the room. The situation was one where words seemed unlikely to help. Sophie continued to weep. Gemma dried her own tears and tried to take stock. Jim was still angry but silent. Damien released his mother from his embrace.

"I don't think any of us is in the mood to talk, let alone eat," he said, his voice steady. "At the risk of getting drunk, I'm going to order more drinks all round and then get them to order a taxi to take us home. This is too much to take in for me. I don't know about you. It's not every day you discover you have a brother who is nearly twenty-five years older than you are – or twenty-five younger, in Jim's case." He got up and went to order more drinks. No one tried to stop him.

The revelations had been such that no one could think of anything to say. Despite his apparent fury, Jim remained silent for fear that what he said would be misinterpreted and hurt everybody, possibly himself. Gemma was the only one whose involvement was less than complete. Acquiring a new brother-in-law was certainly surprising, but far less shocking than the acquisition of a new brother. Her head was still clear enough for a while for her to wonder what the relationship was between her new friend, Sophie, and Jim – hardly a step-mother, that would be weird. As for how the four of them would come to terms with all this, she could not even hazard a guess.

Thus, a very strange, virtually dumb group clambered into a taxi and drove homewards.

For the second time that week Gemma woke with a hangover. Jim's side of the bed was empty, so she went to the small bathroom to fetch a glass of water. She had almost to push her husband out of the way. Neither of them spoke. Gemma walked as far as the bed, groped for the remaining painkillers in her handbag, swallowed the last two and emptied the glass. She felt awful as the events of the previous evening returned to her consciousness. She was still sitting on the side of the bed when Jim returned. He still did not speak but dressed. The atmosphere was tense. He left the bedroom, still silent, and Gemma went back to the shower. Her head throbbed. She dressed painfully. It was 9 o'clock.

Downstairs, Jim was drinking coffee. He barely looked up when his wife entered. He did not meet her eyes. Jean came in and asked what Gemma wanted for breakfast. The very thought of food made her feel worse, however, and she asked for a slice of bottom toast and some tea. Jean gave her a sympathetic glance and went off to get it. The couple must have had a hard night, she imagined.

"I want to go home as soon as you are finished," Jim announced. "I'll start the packing." And with that he headed back upstairs. The thought of two or three hours in the car was almost enough to put Gemma off her meagre breakfast, but she persevered before following her husband. His idea of packing was haphazard but she could not be bothered to complain, nor was she prepared to re-do what he had already started. She tucks the overhanging pieces of clothing into the suitcase, folded her own clothes as neatly as she could, thinking she would deal with them when she got home. Jim, fortunately, left her to it. Toiletries and other oddments were thrown into the smaller bag. She left the suitcase for Jim to carry down.

Jean had been expecting them to stay one more night. She said as much has Jim took out his wallet and paid her in cash for the week. He ignored her protests at the over-payment, waving them away. He did not look happy. Jean was concerned for them both, telling them to drive carefully. By 10 o'clock they were on the road. They had still not spoken. Several times Gemma opened her mouth to speak, but did not know where to begin and instead opened her window a few inches, hoping the wind would alleviate the pain behind her eyes. Her action provoked a response from Jim.

"Can you shut that blasted window? "He said curtly. "It's making a draft."

Meekly, Gemma did as asked and sank into the seat with her eyes closed. She was telling herself she would never drink alcohol again. The journey continued. After a long time she felt the car slowed down. She opened her eyes and saw they were pulling into a service station.

"I need a wee ." Jim explained, almost the only words he had spoken.

"Do they do coffees?" Gemma asked, but Jim was already on his way across the forecourt. Reluctantly she entered the small shopping area. There was a coffee machine and she scrabbled in her bag for the cash. Deliberately, she bought only one. Jim said nothing as he climbed back into the driving seat.

"We'll need to stop and buy some supplies," Gemma pointed out. "The fridge is empty."

Jim scowled. "When we get home," he said.

Gemma said no more, struggling not to spill the coffee in the cardboard mug. She glanced at her husband. He was staring intensely at the road ahead, his face set in a grim expression that was so unusual it scared her. She looked away, wondering how this dreadful journey would end. Jim was like a growing thunderstorm, about to split open in a huge thunderclap. If not now, thought Gemma, once they reached the familiar seclusion of their house. She had grown to love their home. They had shared many years furnishing it with bits and pieces they had collected on their numerous holidays. It was literally full of memories. The prospect of an emotional storm which was gathering made her shrink. She remained silent as the miles were covered and the sights and sounds of their home town brought them to Tesco. Jim did not leave the car. Gemma collected milk, bread, cereals, and ingredients for a couple of easy meals. She put them in the car and Jim drove the short distance home. They let themselves in. Jim took the cases upstairs. Gemma put the food away, opened the curtains and windows. In the kitchen she filled a kettle and made some tea. It was 2.30.

At last Jim joined her. She poured a mug of tea and pushed it across the table.

"All right," she said. "Let's have it."

Jim looked at her and frowned. "What? "he asked.

"You've had a face like a thundercloud all day. You're clearly furious with me Tell me exactly what I've done wrong."

But he did not reply. Instead, he took a great gulp of his tea, slammed the mug down on the table so hard that a small amount splashed out, then he stood up and turned towards the sitting room door. "Gemma," he said, "you're not stupid. Don't pretend you are. You know perfectly well why I'm upset."

He left the room. Gemma followed. He was in the conservatory. He had taken out his precious binoculars to watch the birds in the garden.

"Any reasonable man," she said, "what I understand and be grateful to discover a long lost brother."

He swung round at that and gazed at her. This time he did not disguise his anger.

"Have you the foggiest idea what you have stirred up?" he asked.

"If I haven't, it's because you have never spoken to me about these things. I don't remember your talking about your time in Fallowfield ever."

"It was an unhappy time," he said. "But that isn't the problem. I didn't like my father. In fact I hated him, but I didn't know he was a paedophile."

"But nor did I. You must understand that."

If you haven't stirred up all this information, I need never have known," Jim said.

"And you can't blame me for that." Gemma was no quite angry herself. She was not prepared to be blamed for her accidental discoveries. "Whatever your father was

Sophie was his victim. Neither you nor I was aware of that fact. You can't blame me for it."

"I wish to God we had never gone back to Fallowfield."

"That's the other thing," Gemma persisted, "at least one good thing came out of this: you have found your brother, your brother," she repeated. "Don't you realise how important that is? Damien is a presentable young man. He must be quite a strong personality. After all, he was an illegitimate child brought up by a single mother. That must have taken some courage."

"And you're going to tell me next," Jim said, "that he must be a very clever young man."

Gemma stared at him, trying to understand his opinions. "Yes, that's true. To get a post at university at his age is quite something. I know accounting isn't the same thing, but surely it means you have something in common?"

"Something in common?" Jim repeated the phrase with what sounded like bitterness. Once more, Gemma was baffled.

"I realise he's only half your age," she said, " your younger brother, and I understand that you don't really know him yet, but I would think you should be proud of him."

Jim did not reply, but shook his head as though he knew his wife would not understand. The anger had faded a little from his face, replaced by an expression of deep regret. Gemma's anger was also subsiding. She did not understand what her husband was going through, but he was clearly deeply distressed. How she had caused that, she did not know, other than revealing a formerly unknown truth. She had always believed that it was better to know the truth than to be in ignorance. This quarrel suggested she was wrong. She stepped forward and put a hand on her husband's arm. He ignored it and turned the other way.

"Jim, please," she said, "talk to me. Explain what this is all about. I really don't understand. I never intended to hurt you and I still don't know how or why I did."

After a while he turned back towards her. "All right," he said. "You may as well know the whole truth." He gestured towards a chair and they both sat face-to-face.

"At the age of 18," he began, "I was a very lonely boy. My father was Deputy head of the school where I was a pupil. It is always hard for a pupil when his father or mother is a teacher on the same staff – or at least it used to be. I made virtually no friends. Perhaps the others were scared I would tell tales at home. Nothing could have been further from the truth. Home was. When my parents taught at all they were bickering part of the time, fighting angry the rest of it. My mother was clearly afraid of my father and I hated him for that."

"What about your mother?"

"It hadn't occurred to me until this trip to Fallowfield's how much younger than my father she was. I suppose I should have noticed when she died. She must be one of his conquests. She must have been still in her teens when I was born."

"Did no one realise?"

"Obviously not. In fact I hadn't really noticed or thought about it until this week. His behaviour explains a lot. I never really understood what the quarrels were about, only that they were full of hate and on my mother's side fear. She was afraid of him. He must have been seducing other young girls all the time. Sophie was the only one who was obviously noticed or, at least, the only one that led to any kind of action. I had no idea of any of this. I buried myself in work – I was quite good at most things except sport. I was especially good at maths and Mr Jenkins encouraged me. He was confident I would go on to university, probably to follow an academic career. I believed him. After all he was the only one who really supported me in all that unpleasant time."

Gemma was listening attentively. "And then you moved."

"It came out of the blue. Nobody explained. I tried to ask my parents but got nowhere. My mother was already in a strange, unstable state of mind, liable to collapse into hysterics at the slightest provocation. My father simply threatened me. I never knew why we moved.

All I did know was that my hopes of getting to university had been completely smashed."

"Why? Surely you could have tried in your new place?"

" I suppose, had I known the roots, I might have done, but life was worse, not better now I had left school and had no friends, no support, no Mr Jenkins. I thought I had been very brave to go to the local Technical College without telling my father and then rolling for a course in bookkeeping. Now I know why he was obliged to move, now his foul secret was out, he must have been in a very unsettled state of mind himself. He chose largely to ignore me. My mother turned into a weakling. I had little sympathy for her. I concentrated on seeking excellence in my bookkeeping course."

"And then your father...?"

"He was a perfectly good driver. There was nothing wrong with this car. When he drove at high speed – yes, high-speed – into a stone bridge, I had my suspicions. My mother was hysterical as usual. The coroner's report assumed he had simply lost control. I was an absolute shambles, a mixture of suspicion, guilt, relief. I have no real sympathy for my mother and within a few weeks she was sectioned. I was left trying to sort out the problems that followed my father's death. I had to settle the mortgage as well as coping with investigators and doctors, and I was only just 21 years old."

"I wish you had told me all this before."

Jim looked at her in helpless despair. "This happened three years before we met," he said. "By then I was on top of it, or I thought I was. My only wish was to put it all behind me, to start again. We were making plans, if you remember people both ambitious. My bookkeeping had turned into accountancy and I could see a way of qualifying."

"That was important to you, wasn't it?"

"You never knew how important. At the age of 18 I had one, glorious dream of winning a place at university where I would distinguish myself as a brilliant mathematician. I had been left with an inferior choice. At the least I could do that."

"And you have done well. You have your own business. It's growing. Your clients respect you and rely on you…"

Jim stood up abruptly and walked towards the windows. "You simply don't understand," he said. "You still don't understand, do you?"

"No. I don't know what it is I'm supposed to understand."

"You and your new friend, Sophie, presented me with a completely unknown brother this week. You both expected me to be rejoicing. Here was a young man, full of vitality, good-looking and clever, and academic success! It's Damien who has the teaching post at the University, Damien, not me. Yet Damien is the accidental outcome of an illegitimate liaison between my hateful father and Sophie. I am supposed to admire him? I find it almost impossible even to accept him. You don't seem to understand any of this. I have every reason to be bitter."

After a while Gemma spoke. "So," she said, "this is what it all boils down to, is it? Playing jealousy, or is it envy? I never knew which is which."

Jim rounded on her at that. "Did you hear what I said?"

"Yes. You pointed out that Sophie and your father broke the law when they produced Damien."

"Well, they clearly did."

"From what you've told me," Gemma said calmly, "it seemed pretty likely the same is true in your case too."

It was clearly a thought which had never crossed Jim's mind. He stared at his wife, speechless.

"It would certainly explain why your parents were constantly fighting throughout your childhood," Gemma pointed out. "You did have a very rough time of it and you did so well to overcome all those problems as you did. I am even more proud of you than I was before. You have succeeded in the face of tremendous odds and with very little support. What you don't seem able to do is understand that Damien has been obliged to face problems of his own. He was brought up without a father at all, probably with our very much money, with the taint of illegitimacy. You have both done well, don't you understand? If I can be proud of you? Why can't you be proud of your own brother?"

"Because he has what I wanted."

"What about the things you have? You have me and we have shared it 20 years together."

"It's not the same thing."

"No, it's not. Of course it's not. But, now you have explained all this, you are going to have to come to terms with the situation. You can't continue feeling resentment and bitterness toward your own brother. He doesn't deserve it." She paused to allow this to sink in, then added, "and, much though I love you, I must say seeing you full of self-pity is not pretty."

She left him then. Not wanting to stay any longer and risk further conversation, she retrieved her own small sports car from the garage where it had been parked for the week. She would recharge the battery by taking the car for a spin and call at the supermarket for a proper shopping visit.

In the kitchen of her small flat in Fallowfield Sophie looked up as Damien appeared.

"How are you feeling?" she asked. She poured him a tumbler full of water and passed it to him. "I'll make some fresh coffee," she said.

Damien sat down "remind me never to drink brandy again," he said.

"I was not referring to your hangover," Sophie said. "I've got one myself. I meant how do you feel about last night. And what do you think of Jim?"

"Jim? Well, I don't really know him, do I? He's a middle-aged man, twice my age. First impressions? He seems, well, morose."

"Morose?"

"To be honest, ma'am," he said taking seat on one of the stalls, "I was much more interested in what I learned about my father."

Sophie winced, as though he had wounded her.

"He sounds like a real bastard."

"He was a very charming man when he wanted to be."

"Until she thought what he wanted, you mean?"

"Maybe. He got his comeuppance in the end."

"Is that what you call it? He lost his job. I bet you he went on to groom other young girls."

"We don't know that. He died, you realise? Drove his car into a wall."

"Leaving quite a mess behind him. Seems to have been his habit. You have never told me anything about this. How did you survive when he disappeared?"

"I was lucky. Once your grandparents got over the shock, they were very supportive. Your grandad was very angry at first, angry with me, that is, called me a stupid little girl. He was right."

"But you decided to keep me?"

"Of course! No one ever suggested anything else. I left school, found a job as an apprentice hairdresser for a few months, and had a baby. We all love to."

"Sorry, mum, this must be very upsetting for you."

"I should have told you all about it years ago. I was too ashamed." Sophie was in the distress. She mopped up her tears on her apron. Damien got off his stool and held her in his arms. He was much taller than his mother.

"Sorry," he said. "It has been a bad experience, all this."

"Yes," she said, her voice muffled as she pressed against his chest.

"But you should never be ashamed," he said gently. "You were only 15 years old. You mustn't waste the rest of your life in regret. I couldn't have wanted a better mother."

After a bit she pulled away from him and turned back to brew the coffee.

"What are you going to do about Jim?" she" asked.

"Do about him? What you mean? He exists. I can't make him go away."

"I meant do you intend to contact him, talk to him?"

Damien shrugged. "I doubt it," he said. "I doubt if we have very much in common other than our dubious history."

"Oh!"

"Why? What difference does it make you?"

"It might be awkward."

"Awkward? In what way?"

"Well, it's not so much Jim as Gemma. I know I don't know her that well, but I like her. I'd like to be her friend."

"So, what has Jim got to do with that?"

"Don't be naïve, Damien. It will be very difficult to be Gemma's friend without bumping into her husband."

"Que sera sera."

"You really won't object?"

"It's none of my business, mum. From what I saw of her, I quite liked Gemma. It's odd, but you and she must be much of the same age."

It was true, Sophie realised. She had not thought in terms of ages. She, Gemma and

Jim must all be similar in age. Damien was very much the odd man out. However, she was glad that her son was not going to object to the continuing friendship. He was an intelligent young man, that she knew well. If he was not especially drawn to his older brother, whom he described as morose, he was bright enough to find the means to handle the relationship, should he need to.

"Tell me about the new job," she said.

"What you want to know? I don't think you really have much understanding of advanced mathematics,, sorry, mum."

"No, you know that's all beyond the. What does lecturing involve? Does it mean you will be standing in front of the hall full of undergraduates or something, passing on your knowledge?"

"No. I may have to take some small classes, a bit like school in many ways."

"What about your research? Are you going to have to give that up? I never did understand how you do research in maths. It's not like there's lots of new stuff to discover, surely Gemma"

Damien laughed. "You're absolutely wrong there," he said. "It's mathematicians that actually lead the way," he said. "It's mathematicians that forecast all kinds of discoveries, like the existence of new planets. In some ways mathematical research is more like philosophy. We are now exploring what time is all about or even if it really exists."

Sophie stared at him, uncomprehending. "Well, it's all beyond me," she said.

"The professor will want me to continue with my research," Damien said. "It's going to be even harder, keeping up with my PhD work as well as teaching."

"So you will be teaching?"

"Oh yes. I'll probably be assigned a number of students that I have to tutor."

"What about getting to the University? It's going to be awkward, relying on buses."

"I've been thinking about that. I think I'm going to have to buy a car."

"Oh!" Sophie looked worried.

"I didn't tell you," Damien reassured her, "Granddad has already suggested he could help. I only need a second-hand thing. I suppose it needs to be reliable. Anyway, you needn't worry. I'm afraid you're stuck with me as a lodger for a while yet."

"That's fine. And it's good of Granddad to help."

"We shall just have to try not to cramp one another's style," Damien said with a grin.

Later that same day Sophie answered her phone.

"Sophie, it's Gemma."

"Gemma! Hello."

"I'm sorry we rushed off like that." Sophie was puzzled. The taxi had dropped Gemma and her husband at their bread and breakfast lodgings after the meeting. They have not seemed to be in any great haste, in fact they were picking their way carefully up the driveway, conscious they had had a great deal to drink.

"Rushed off? What do you mean?"

"I think I'd better start again. We are back home. Jim insisted on driving back today rather than tomorrow. This whole business has upset him."

"You are home?"

"Well, at the moment, I'm sitting in my car in a lay by. I've had what you might call a discussion with Jim, trying to talk some sense into him. I thought it might be sensible for me to get out into the countryside for some fresh air, clear my head. I just wanted to let you know what was happening. I wouldn't normally have dashed away like that without saying goodbye."

"Oh, now I understand. I'm glad you rang. I don't know how you feel exactly, but I certainly want to keep in touch."

"Oh good! That's the way I feel, too. It looks like it will have to be by phone for the moment. I can't see myself travelling down to

Fallowfield in the near future and I don't imagine you will want to come up here."

"No, I'm too busy. I work on Saturdays as well. That's not a bad thing in many ways, but it would be nice to have the occasional weekend off, other than bank holidays."

"And in any case you wouldn't want to be driving all the way up here."

"I don't drive. I don't have a car. Damien is about to buy one with help from his grandfather, but I can't really see him driving me all the way out there. It will have to be the phone, I'm afraid."

"So long as we keep in touch, that's all that matters."

Jim, meanwhile, had been attempting to get back to work without much success. He was unable to concentrate. He turned his attention on the garden, but he simply could not settle. He was unaccountably restless and he felt there was something wrong which she could not identify. Gemma had definitely upset him, left him feeling there was something wrong, but he was not at all sure what the problem was. She did not understand how the revelation of a brother, or even her half brother, could be so profoundly disturbing. For Jim, it felt as though Fate had told him another cruel blow. It was not Damien's existence which in itself disturbed him, rather, it was the knowledge that Damien was a gifted mathematician – gifted enough to have secured a teaching post in the University. It was simply not fair. He had nothing in common with this young man. Damien was not only half his age, he was unmarried and had been brought up by Sophie, a single mother. Judging by their apparent relationship, he had not wanted for love, at least from his mother. And he was rewarded by his new job. No, it was certainly not fair.

The telephone rang. He picked it up, expecting it to be one of his clients. Instead, a less familiar voice asked, "is that Jim Grainger?"

"Yes," he replied uncertainly. "Who's calling?"

"Bernard Jenkins. I wasn't sure if I'd got the number right. I scribbled it down in a hurry. My sight is not what it used to be."

"Mr Jenkins! Nice of you to ring."

"Since we had that little chat," said his old teacher, "I have been worrying about you are a little. "You seem to be unsettled. It's not surprising. Are you still in Fallowfield?"

"No. I decided to come home early."

"Oh, that's a pity. I was hoping we could meet again before you left. What made you change your mind?"

Jim realised that Mr Jenkins only knew half the story. He told him of the meeting which Gemma had arranged with a woman called Sophie and her son and how Damien's identity had been revealed.

Bernard Jenkins was very surprised. He remembered Sophie as a young girl. He remembered that she was the girl who had been named as being involved in the scandalous affair with Jack Grainger, but he did not know what had happened to Sophie. News of her pregnancy came as a shock. The realisation that Damien, her son, was Jim's half-brother, came to him instantly.

"Oh my goodness!" he said. "That must have come as a real shock. "

"Yes. I am still trying to come to terms with it," Jim said.

"But this young man must be, let me see, over 20 years old.

"He's still only half my age."

"Yes, I can understand that. Does he have a job?"

Jim hesitated. "That's the most awful thing about it," he said.

"Why?"

Jim explained that Damien had just landed a job as a mathematics lecturer.

"A lecturer in mathematics? Another mathematician? It obviously runs in the family."

"Can you begin to understand how I feel about that?"

"Tell me."

Jim spilled out his bitterness.

"I see," Bernard Jenkin commented.

"It's so, bloody unfair!"

"I suppose that's one way of describing it."

"Surely you don't disagree?"

"Jim," I can understand a little of how you feel, "but a long, long time ago I learned that life has nothing to do with fairness. If you allow ideas of fairness or even of justice to dominate your thinking, you end up in a very unhappy person. I know how much you wanted to go to university when you were young man. Now you have this – I was going to say mirror image of yourself who has been given this opportunity. You mustn't allow yourself to become jealous of your own brother."

"That seems to be what Gemma thinks."

"And it's very sensible. I hope I can get to know Gemma."

"You know," said Jim, "I thought you, of all people, what understand where I'm coming from."

"Of course I understand," Bernard Jenkin's said. "Remember, I spent 40 years of my life teaching maths to children. The highest I ever climbed was teaching A level. I never had the opportunity to climb any further, much though I'd have liked to"

"I'm sorry. It never occurred to me."

"You know, Jim, a writer, Gustav Flaubert, once writing about one of his characters, said 'It's the story of an unfulfilled life, but all lives are unfulfilled more or less'. I believe he had a point."

The line was silent for a long time, then Jim said, "Well, I have always respected your opinions, but this time you'll have to forgive me if I disagree."

"Are you going to allow this kind of bitterness to affect your relationship with – what's his name? – Damien?"

"At the moment I don't think I want anything to do with him."

"Oh dear! That would be a terrible shame. Apart from his interest in maths, he is your brother. It will be hugely interesting to get to know him. I'm sure you would like him, if you could ditch your prejudices."

"We'll see," Jim said. "He did not sound optimistic."

"I do hope you change your mind. It sounds as though it will be up to you to make the necessary advances. He lives a long way from you, after all. He is not only going to be busy, settling into a new job, making friends, he will probably not be very well off. Travelling may be something he can't really afford. But he has a wonderful career to pursue. You could have a wonderful relationship to discover and despite the age difference, you could enjoy getting to know him. As the older brother you would have a great deal to offer him, too. How does Gemma feel about this?"

"We haven't talked a great deal about it, but I think she feels much the same way as you do."

"This has all been more than I expected. It's not really my business, but I do hope you change your mind."

"Not likely at the moment, I'm afraid."

"Do you mind if I keep in touch?"

"Of course not. We may disagree on this, but I all looked up to you as a kind of mental."

"That is very kind of you. Maybe I should talk to your wife!"

"That's how I feel about it at the moment. Gemma's gone for a drive. I'm sure she'd like to talk to you, but I hope you don't intend to gang up on me."

"Gang up on you? What a thing to suggest!"

"But thank you for ringing."

"I take it that his permission to continue as your mentor."

"My mentor, yes, but no bullying."

"My dear boy! I have never been a bully in my life."

All the same, Jim thought as the call ended, Bernard Jenkins was one of several people in the queue that disagreed with him. He was under pressure. Gemma was behaving oddly. He cursed as he assessed yet again the problems which had resulted from the Fallowfield trip. Gemma had said very little before she set off for work after a week away.

She should have been refreshed by the break but the opposite seemed to be the case.

"I'm going to move into the spare bedroom," she said. "I'm sleeping badly."

She had offered no other explanation. Jim was surprised, would have preferred to discuss the idea, but Gemma was in a hurry to get back to work. The plan to move out of the marital bedroom was worse than unexpected; it implied a serious change in their relationship. Their sex life had always been satisfying and enjoyed by both. He had been taken aback, even hurt when Gemma had rebuffed him in Fallowfield. He had not mentioned the fact then, but now, given other differences between them, it was desirable to talk about this new turn. They had always discussed everything fully ad openly. This was probably something they could sort out. Jim felt an unusual sensation which took a while to identify; it was a kind of fear and he recognised an emotion from his adolescent years. In his late teens in school where he had no friends and at home with warring parents the overriding background had been fear, or maybe it was profound loneliness. Gemma's announcement that she would no longer share his bed reawakened a similar taste of loneliness. He did not want to be alone again. He pulled himself together and opened the door to the drinks cabinet, poured a large whisky and took a mouthful. He felt it burn its way down to his stomach. After a short time, it dulled his senses. He poured a second, then sat heavily in a large chair and fell asleep. He woke with a thick head at four in the afternoon.

Meanwhile, Gemma drove herself to work. She was tired. By choice her job was largely routine but she was content with that. Today she was not looking forward to returning to the same procedures, not even particularly interested in mixing with her colleagues. She felt restless as well as tired. The week in Fallowfield was too short. She parked her car and walked in to the office. Her desk was at the back of a large, open plan room. Even before she had taken of her coat, she could see the in tray was piled high. Normally she would have been interested to see which properties had sold and who it was that was buying them. Today she just saw a great deal of work awaiting her. Her colleagues seemed genuinely pleased to see her but the smile she gave them in return felt false. She sat down at her computer and logged in. She not only found that she lacked interest, she found it difficult to concentrate. Several times she got up to make herself coffee but then found she was having to take frequent breaks to go to the toilet. She felt vaguely uncomfortable. By 4 o'clock in the afternoon she had developed a headache. She explained herself to her boss who told her to go home. The headache was getting worse and she was relieved to let herself in. Jim was upstairs in his office so she went into the sitting room with a glass of water, kicked off her shoes and laid down on the sofa.

Jim had heard her come in. "Your home early." Gemma felt it unnecessary to reply to such a statement of the obvious.

"I'm glad you are home early," Jim began again. "I think we should talk about this idea of yours of sleeping in the spare room."

"Oh Jim!" Not know!" Gemma was uncharacteristically irritable. "Can't you see I've got a headache?"

"I'm sorry. Can I get you anything?"

"No. Just go away and close the door behind you."

He stared at her. Gemma was normally easy-going and tolerant. He turned and left the room.

Chapter Three

Gemma fell asleep after a while and woke up feeling cramped. She turned on a lamp and found it was 7 o'clock. For a moment she thought it might be seven in the morning, but she thought up and went to the kitchen where the 24-hour clock read 19. 10. She filled the kettle to make tea she then realised there were dishes in the sink. Jim had made himself soup. She loaded the dirty dishes into the dishwasher. One of the glasses smelled strongly of whiskey. That was unusual. She made herself some toast and a mug of tea. Jim was presumably in his office but she did not venture into the bedroom. Instead, she stripped to her underwear and climbed into one of the single beds which she had made up the previous day. She was glad to be on her own, not to have two speak to her husband before breakfast.

It was a restless night. The few hours she had spent on the sofa might have taken the edge off her need to sleep. She tossed and turned on the unfamiliar bed. Each time she woke she thought the headache had disappeared until she moved. Finally she was awake and the little, bedside clock and told her it was 6 AM. She got up, risked waking her husband, and retrieve some clean underwear before taking a long shower. She stepped out and took the warm bath towel and wrapped it round herself. She looked up to see Jim in the doorway. She had no false modesty. They had seen one another naked many times, but Jim's presence felt like an intrusion and she looked at him.

"So, you meant it!" Jim said.

She continued to stare at him, uncomprehending.

"Moving into the spare room," he explained.

"Oh, Jim! Can't I even have a shower in peace? I've only just woken up. It looks as though you haven't slept well either."

"What do you expect?" But he left her to finish drying herself and dressing.

This strange antagonism and tension continued through breakfast. Gemma phoned the office to say she was still not feeling well, maybe it was flu, but it would be best if she did not come in. Then she turned to her husband and said, "All right. Let's talk, if you think it will do any good."

"I want to know what's going on," Jim said. "Surely, finding out that I have a half-brother isn't the main problem? I am bewildered. What's going on?"

"I don't know. I really don't know. Things have changed and I don't know why. It had nothing to do with your brother, at least, so far as I know. I think you're wrong to dismiss his existence like this, but that's not at the bottom of the way I feel."

"Don't you think I deserve an explanation?"

Gemma nodded. "Yes, you do. So do I. I tell you, I don't know what this is all about. It's just that suddenly I feel quite differently about you. Don't ask me to explain. I can't. It's as though you are just, well, any man. I know you're my husband but I don't have the same kind of feelings toward you. It's as though something has snapped."

"That can't be true, not after all the time we have spent together. We've built a life together. What are you trying to tell me, that it all over?"

"I don't know. I keep telling you, I don't know. I don't know if this is some queer, temporary thing which will end up with some kind of pressure reunion, but it certainly doesn't feel like that at the moment."

"And I am supposed to be happy with that, and I?"

Gemma shrugged. "You talk as though I have some motive. I don't. I haven't wished this on, me you, on both of us. It just seems to have happened. I don't know how you are supposed to react. This weird change is just as difficult for me."

"You must be joking! You sit there, cool as a cucumber, telling me that I'm supposed to accept your decision to return to being to, single persons after 20 years of being married, and I get no choice in this at all? You can't expect me to accept it just like that."

Gemma sighed. "I do feel sorry for you," she said. "Clearly this is a terribly difficult thing to accept. It feels a complete change in my feelings"

"So, who decided you should sleep in a different bed?"

"That's not what I meant, and you know it. I meant this – for me it's a

"What on earth is that supposed to mean?"

"I don't have any feelings."

"You mean, you have become an automaton all at once?"

"That's one way of putting it. Look, Jim, I think the only hope you have is to be patient. I can't promise – I don't know – whether this sudden change in me is permanent or not. It is not a conscious act on my part aimed at hurting you. It might, as I said, be temporary."

"You don't even seem to understand just how devastating this is for me. You have been my life for the past 20 years. Now I'm supposed to wait indefinitely for you to change back. And I have no say in this, no control, no rights.

Everything is down to you. I have always been able to talk to you, knowing that you love me, believed in me, that you were on my side, so to speak. It's as though you have removed the main support."

He got up and turned away. Gemma saw tears on his cheek and she felt immense pity to see his suffering. She also felt guilty that she was responsible. Talking, it seemed, was not likely to achieve very much. What should she do next? To leave completely would appear to be the logical thing to do but moving out would surely appear to be a sign, an acknowledgement that this was final. Whas her marriage over? She was not terribly concerned about that. Jim, as he pointed out, did not deserve this pain. It was she, Gemma, who was inflicting it. If she stayed, on the other hand, would she be giving him false hope? Never in her life had she been faced with such a profoundly difficult choice. If only she unerstood her own feelings or lack of them, she might take a rational decision. She continued to sit in the comfortable kitchen in silent thought. She had the door open and close: Jim had gone out. She stepped outside as his car drove off. She thought about his statement that she was his principal support and it struck her that he might have no one to talk to, someone who could at least sympathise, even if unable to understand. As for herself, well, she had one or two friends, including Sophie now. She felt she would survive this very difficult moment, come what may, but she could not be sure of Jim. He had probably gone off to watch birds. She turned back indoors. She felt fairly weak and wondered if her recent a migraine had anything to do with it. She decided she would see the doctor.

She was obliged to wait three weeks for an appointment so, when the time came, she had almost forgotten. She felt a little foolish, not sure exactly how to describe her symptoms. The doctor, a woman, was not a GP she you, making it even more difficult, but she explained that she had been having migraines, felt rundown and depressed. The doctor asked about her general health and took a very short time to diagnose the problem.

"It seems very clear to me," she said, "that you are beginning them menopause."

"I am only 44," Gemma protested.

"A little early, perhaps, but some women start the menopause even earlier. It certainly sounds like it in your case."

"What have I got to look forward to?"

"You may need to consider HRT," said the doctor. "But it will be an unsettling time." She found a pamphlet from among the many on a small display stand and gave it to Gemma. "Take this away and read it and come back to me if you have any questions, especially about HRT. The menopause is I'm afraid, a normal part of a woman's experience. The blood test and the urine sample will help confirm the initial diagnosis. If I am right, it will probably take some time to run its course. You will not suffer all the symptoms described at once. Just do not get too alarmed."

Gemma came away with mixed feelings. Some of her symptoms were simply explained. They included the loss of libido. The low moods which had been playing her of late were also probably a result of changes in her hormones. At least she had an explanation, but the condition will unlikely to change very much. As for hormone replacement therapy, she had heard it could increase her vulnerability to cancer. She would have to take it into account. Without it, however, the lows might well continue or even get worse. All this, she thought, with an unaccustomed resentment was happening at a time when she needed the emotional support of her husband. Then her sense of fairness reminded her that she was failing him just as he was failing her. She was left feeling depressed.

The decision they have made so many years ago not to have children would, they knew, have very serious consequences. They had discussed these as best we could, acknowledging as young people in their 20s they might be mistaken. One such consequence was the lack of excitement to be shared with children at Christmas. On balance, both Gemma and Jim thought the freedom to spend Christmas how and where they wished could largely make up for the fun of warnings surrounded by excited children, wrapping paper and city toys. Ever since the decision had been made, they had chosen exciting venues, mostly overseas. Furthermore, children, they also calculated, were expensive all year round. They had both chosen to concentrate on pursuing their careers. They not only had a money to spend on overseas holidays, they also settled into a comfortable house and a self-indulgent lifestyle. Now that the relationship between them had cooled abruptly, neither of them was much inclined to want to travel. Their experience in Fallowfield put them off. The house remained comfortable, but they tried to avoid one another much of the time. It was now a house rather than a home. Indeed, Jim spent less and less time at home when he was not working. He developed the habit of packing sandwiches and his binoculars and driving off to the less well inhabited areas, woods, lakes, rivers, wildlife reserves, even on occasion mountainous areas, staying away for two or three nights at a time.

So it was that Gemma was left alone one cold, blustery weekend. Dark clouds studied overhead and released occasional bursts of rain or hail. She decided to call Sophie. They had not spoken for some time. Sophie seemed remarkably cheerful and was delighted by the call. They exchanged the usual, meaningless comments about the weather, then Gemma said that she felt she needed to get away. Jim was aware until Monday, she explained. He was busy watching birds at some wetland area. She, Gemma, thought she might drive down to Fallowfield and say hello. Sophie was delighted by the idea. She pointed out it would be an unpleasant drive in the wind and the rain, but Gemma could cope. She gave Jean a call. Jean would make up a bed for her with pleasure. Within an hour Gemma put up the hood on her little car, stowed a grip on the back seat, and set off. She always kept the car in good condition and was an experienced driver. The most unpleasant part of the journey was whenever a great wave of water was thrown over her small vehicle by the lorries which overtook her. It was nevertheless better than moping indoors. Gemma was aware of the depression that weighed constantly on her brain. It lifted perceptibly when Jean greeted her with a hot cup of tea.

Sophie had warned her she was working until 6 pm, so Gemma walked to the salon to meet her. The rain had stopped, though there were still occasional gusts of wind. The salon was still lit and Gemma went in.

"Gemma! Good to see you! Nearly finished," Sophie said. The customer in the chair gave an uncertain smile. "Take a seat," Sophie said, turning back to the client.

"Sorry I'm running late," Sophie said as she turned the key in the lock. "I don't know if you've eaten but I'm starving. What about fish and chips?" They had only to walk a few steps, and they walked home like two teen-agers on a night out. Sophie's flat was a short distance. The kitchen-living room provided a table on which to open the warm packages. Sophie opened a bottle of wine to go with the food. Gemma had forgotten how lively and energetic she was. They ate in silence at first.

"That's what I like about it," said Sophie, as she threw the empty cardboard boxes in the bin,"No washing up! Now, let's make ourselves comfy and you can tell me all the news."

Gemma, to her utter dismay, suddenly burst into tears.

"Oh, Gemma! Whatever is the matter?"

Gemma was unable to reply. The weeping had hold of her. She had no idea what she was crying for, she was simply overwhelmed by grief. Sophie was helpless. She had no idea what this was about and could do nothing but wait. Neither of them noticed during this torrent of tears that the door opened as Damien returned home. He took two steps into the room and then stopped and waited like his mother for the storm to subside.

"I am so sorry," Gemma said at last, accepting a box of tissues which Sophie held out to her. "I don't know what that was about. How very embarrassing!"

"Was it something I said, Gemma?"

"No." Gemma blew her nose vigorously. "It's the menopause."

Sophie had no reply to this. Behind Gemma, Damien coughed discreetly. Gemma was embarrassed all over again. Her embarrassment took the form of a hot flush. Her face and neck and shoulders burned and she leaned forward, holding several tissues to her face as she waited for the heat to fade. Damien took advantage of the pause to slip past as far as the kitchen where he made himself a drink and perched on a stool in an attempt to be unobtrusive. They were silent for several minutes.

"How very embarrassing!" Gemma said at last. "I'm so sorry!"

"There's no need to be sorry," said Sophie, but she was at a loss, not knowing how to deal with this strange phenomenon.

"Can I have a glass of water?"

To her surprise the tumbler full of water was proffered by Damien Gemma tried to apologise to him.

"Don't worry," he said. "I'll make myself scarce. I didn't choose the best time to come home, did I?"

"Don't feel you have to go," Gemma said. "I was looking forward to seeing you again. How are you? How's the new job"

"It's fine. I'm sure you don't really want to talk about that now."

"Can I use your bathroom, and clean myself up? Then I'd love to talk to both of you."

Sophie pointed out the door to the bathroom and left her to wash her face and comb her hair Damien returned to the kitchen and made tea for everybody. Gemma,

"that's better," Gemma said, taking place in an easy chair. Sophie and her son sat on the sofa.

"Well," Sophie began, "you are clearly not well. Don't feel you need to explain, however. Just relax. You are among friends."

Gemma smiled "Thank you," she said. "Not just friends, relations."

Mother and son nodded "have you got used to the idea yet?" The question was addressed to Damien.

"Not really," he said. It seems to have opened up a whole can of worms I knew nothing about my father. In some ways I think that was probably a good thing. It sounds as though he was a pretty awful man. And that worries me, as you might expect. What have I inherited from him? I don't know. What about Jim? How does he feel about all this now? He was obviously very shocked when we first met."

"Well, it looks as though you both inherited something from your father," Gemma said. "I have always admired Jim's ability with figures. And you – well, you must be pretty gifted in that direction."

"There is a bit of difference between mathematics and arithmetic," Damien said. A lot of the work I do has little to do with numbers."

"I understand," said Gemma. "I think I understand, anyway. What I have learned is that Jim, your brother, at your age, or even younger, was more or less obliged to choose a career he didn't really want. Obviously he's got arithmetic, though that is only part of the skill he needs to do his job as an accountant and adviser. What he really wanted was a career at university level. He never had the opportunity."

"That's tough," Damien said. He was genuinely sympathetic. "There must be thousands, no, millions of people who find themselves doing a job they don't really want to do. I am extremely lucky and I know it."

"But you've earned it!" His mother said.

"I have worked at it," Damien admitted, "but I enjoyed it. I still enjoy. It is a privilege for me. I shall always be grateful, so, no matter if my father was a reprobate, he left me a precious gift."

"Perhaps I should explain," Gemma said, "that when I first met your brother he was 24 years old. We were young and in love and not really interested in each other's families. I did know that both Jim's parents were dead. His father had died in a road accident. His mother had suffered from an unspecified illness and died in hospital and this all happened before we actually met. As a result, I knew nothing about Jack, your father, except that he had been a maths teacher. I knew there had been some kind of scandal but that was in the past. It is now even further in the past, of course. "

"So," said Damien with a smile, "I was your skeleton in the cupboard."

Gemma laughed. "Not exactly how I regard it but we didn't even know of your existence."

"The whole business," Sophie said, interrupting the narrative, "was very unusual. I was really a victim, something I did not understand at the time. I thought I was in love with Jack. Later it became clear that he had groomed me, to use the current word. Other people took a stricter view. Remember I was not even 16 years old. I had no rights. Everything was forced upon me. Your father was sent into exile somewhere in the country. I never knew where. My father accepted what I suppose was a bribe and also took me away from Fallowfield where we lived in, and I never heard anything about Jack until the last few weeks. This is all new for all of us."

"The most difficult thing to accept," said Damien, "is not that he was a paedophile, but that you thought you loved him."

"I realise that is hard to understand, but it's not something I can apologise for. Jack was a very charming man. Looking back, maybe I was in part flattered by his attention. At the age of 15 I could not really discriminate, I suppose."

Mother and son looked at one another without speaking for a while.

"Gemma," Damien said at last, "I'm sorry you got dragged into this. It would be nice if he could start again simply as friends."

"Yes, a good idea," said Gemma.

"This is really no way to entertain a guest, mum, it's hardly what you would call Smalltalk, is it?"

"You're right," Sophie agreed. "We should be trying to get to know one another better. We do seem to have plunged in at the deep end."

There was mutual agreement on this point.

"Is Jim not with you?" Damien asked.

"He's gone off for the weekend," Gemma explained. "I don't know if it's simply an excuse to get away. He is birdwatching."

"Birdwatching? I don't think I've ever known anybody who was a birdwatcher. It sounds a bit like Trainspotting."

"I think it is a bit like that," Gemma agreed. "He has a list of birds he might see, and he ticks them off as he sees them."

Both Damien and Sophie looked puzzled by this explanation.

"Has he been doing this for a long time?"

"No, this is a new hobby which he only took up when we came down here a few weeks ago."

"What kind of hobbies do you do together?" Damien asked.

"We travel a lot. We are lucky in that respect. We can both more or less take time off whenever we want. Jim has his own business. It means travelling quite a lot – he's an accountant – and I have a kind of partnership in a firm of solicitors."

"I don't really know what a solicitor does," Damien admitted. "And I'm not exactly sure what an accountant does either. It's a lot more complicated than just bookkeeping, I imagine."

"Oh yes. Of course, he has to be a book keeper for much of the time. The more interesting part of the work is advising his clients on all matters not necessarily financial, helping them to make the right choices and giving knowledgeable advice on things like tax. It means keeping up-to-date with legislation and regulations and that sort of thing."

"Sounds as if it can be quite a rewarding job."

"Yes, I think Jim thought it was too, at least until recently."

Damien said nothing but waited for Gemma to continue.

"Coming down here and confronting his past," Gemma said, upset him in a completely unexpected way. When he was your age or, maybe, even a little younger than you, Jim nursed an ambition to have an academic career. Meeting you, learning about your new job reawakened lots of old wishes and desires. It's not so much that he has discovered he has a brother half his own age, so much as having to accept you are achieving the success he never had. I hate to say this, but he is jealous!"

"But that's ridiculous!"

"I know. It's what I told him."

"Is there anything we can do about it?"

"Sadly, no." And Gemma was clearly upset by the situation. Damien and his mother were finding it hard to understand.

"You know," Damien said after a while, "once I got over the shock I was coming round to the idea that having an older brother could be useful."

"Useful?" Sophie asked.

"Well, he could have introduced me to some of his friends, got me into the golf club, that sort of thing. And it would be good sometimes to get is advice on all kinds of things, like the choice of girlfriends."

Both women laughed at that. The conversation drifted on. Gemma was feeling more at her ease now. She entertained the other two with accounts of the travels and holidays she and Jim had taken. The Sophie did not disguise her envy. Money had always been a problem for her. Some of the faraway places Gemma talked about seemed to both Sophie and her son exotic. It was getting late. Damien insisted on walking Gemma back to her lodgings. She found her key and turned to her brother-in-law.

"Thank you," she said, and gave him a quick kiss on the cheek.

"We'll have to work on Jim," Damien said. "He'll just have to get over his problems and accept the fact that he's got a bigger family than he thought."

"I hope we can sort it out," Gemma said. "We've all got a lot to gain."

She let herself in and went straight to her room.

The rain cleared away overnight, leaving only the threat of showers. Gemma's mood lightened. She ate a little breakfast and drove down to the sea for an hour. She sat and watched the waves . After a while she drove through deserted streets as far as Sophie's flat. She had suggested she might take Sophie and her son out to lunch, but the offer was firmly refused. Sophie wanted to cook for the three of them. It was a simple meal, well cooked. Gemma's sense of wellbeing continued, but she announced she would leave early. She wanted to get home in time to see Jim, she said. She was also aware that Sophie had only two days until she went back to work. She thanked Sophie and Damien for their kindness and began the journey home in mid-afternoon. The roads were almost empty on the Sunday and she made good time, but her mood darkened as the daylight began to fade. She wanted to talk seriously to Jim, but feared his reaction.,.

She arrived before her husband, but she heard his car as it crunched the gravel.

"Oh, you're back," he said.

"Yes, not much traffic."

He nodded.

"Did you have a good time?"

"It was OK," he said.

"Jim, can we go to the sitting room? I have something to talk to you about."

He frowned at that, but followed her into the comfort of the room next door. Before they sat down he went to the drinks cabinet and poured himself half a glass of whisky. Gemma refused a drink. She was concerned that he was drinking. It was new.

"All right," he said, "let's have it."

"Well, first " Gemma began, "I'm sorry I've not been myself ever since we got back from Fallowfield."

"Go on."

"I went to see the doctor this week."

"You're ill? What is it? Serious?" He was all at once very concerned. "No, not really."

"What then?"

"Apparently, I've started the menopause."

Jim stared at her "Thank God!" he said.

His reaction confounded Gemma. "Why 'thank God'?

"I thought you were planning to leave me," he said.

"No, Jim. Though we do need to talk about this. When I moved into the spare room, I realise you were badly hurt. It's down to my hormones. And I'm sorry, but I just can't face the thought of sex at the moment. "

"I'm still not sure what this is all about."

Gemma reached across to a small table and picked up the pamphlet the doctor had given her. "Read this," she said. "These symptoms have begun, hot flushes, night sweats, sudden mood swings, migraine. I can't sleep properly and most of the time I feel depressed." She was crying. Jim moved next to her and put an arm round her.

"And can they do anything about it?! He asked.

"I have another appointment next week," Gemma explained. "They want to do some other tests – they've already taken a blood sample. I shall probably go on HRT treatment.

I don't know if you can understand how I feel about this. It means I've come to the end of - well, I'll never be able to have a child. It's as though part of my value as a woman is finished." Slowly she began to explain as best she could.

At least, thought Gemma, they were talking. She snuggled closer for comfort as the conversation continued and the garden outside was dark.

A long time later, Gemma pulled away and sat up.

"Are you all right?" Jim asked.

"Yes, but there's something else."

"What?"

"I don't really know how you'll think about this."

Jim was virtually invisible in the gloom, but Gemma sensed the way he stiffened.

"What now?" he asked.

"You know I've been down to Fallowfield to see Sophie and Damien?"

"Yes."

"They've had a rough time of it. They have very little money."

"You're not going to suggest we start supporting them somehow?"

"No, but - well, I don't think I'm going to want to go away for Christmas this year. In any case it could well be too late to book anything."

For many years they had flown to a hotel abroad for Christmas. It was easier than organising something at home. Many resorts offered splendid breaks and plenty of company. It had become a normal part of their annual routine.

"So, what are you suggesting/ Please don't say you want to spend more time in Fallowfield"

"No.I just thought maybe we could have Sophie and Damien to stay with us for a day or two."

There was no reply to this at first.

"Jim?"

"I'm not exactly keen on the idea," he said. "But I suppose we've got the room..."

"They live in a poky little flat," Gemma said. "It's nice enough, but it made me think we live in luxury by comparison. It would be a nice gesture. I feel I've struck up a genuine friendship with Sophie and I really like Damien."

There was another silence while Jim thought about it.

"Jim?"

"If you're sure," he said. "We'd better book Christmas lunch somewhere and be quick about it."

"We could try a traditional feast," Gemma said, "cook it all here."

"Sounds like hard work."

"We can get them to help."

"Four of us in the kitchen?"

"Why not?"

"It will all depend on whether Sophie and your brother..." she paused "your brother will want to come."

The next day Gemma rang Sophie with the invitation. Sophie hesitated. She did not like feeling she was being patronised. Could she supply the turkey or some other part of the meal Negotiations continued for several phone calls. Gemma explained that she did very little cooking. Sophie was happy to take charge of the meal, suggested a range of cold items to be prepared in advance. They would drive from Fallowfield on December 23 and the two women would work in the kitchen on Christmas Eve. The men could find something to entertain themselves. Sophie asked if Gemma had any board games to while away Christmas afternoon and was surprised when the answer was no. She would bring an assortment. In return Gemma would provide entertainment for Boxing Day. Separately, they both fretted over presents. The discussions over the phone reinforced their growing friendship

Chapter Four

Gemma began her Hormone Replacement Therapy. It helped. All the symptoms she had begun to experience became a little less severe but they did not disappear entirely. She found it difficult to concentrate on her work and began to make mistakes. This in its turn made her very irritable and she snapped at her colleagues. Frustrated, she spoke to her partner, a man she had known for many years, and suggested she should take time off. He agreed and Gemma took six months' leave. At the end of the six months they would review the situation.

Idleness did not really suit Gemma. She had worked all her adult life. With more time on her hands she did not relax more. Instead, she tended to brood on her situation and her condition. The housekeeper, Mrs Bellingham, came three days a week to keep the large house clean and tidy, leaving little for Gemma to do. Gemma found she was obliged to keep out of the way so as to avoid allowing her own frustration to create friction.

So it was that she was sitting with a book while Mrs Bellingham hoovered in the next room. Gemma was unable to concentrate on the book. She read two pages at a time, then had to reread them. The telephone rang, not her mobile, but the landline. It was a little extravagance, but, since both Gemma and her husband were frequently out at the same time, the landline was quite useful because it gave Jim's clients a means of contacting him. Mrs Bellingham took the call, then brought the handset to Gemma.

"Gemma? It's Bernard Jenkins."

Gemma explained that Jim was out, visiting a client.

"I know," said Mr Jenkins, "it's you I want to talk to."

Gemma sat up.

"To begin with," said Mr Jenkins, "do you think you could call me Bernard? Calling me Mr Jenkins simply reminds me how old I am."

Gemma smiled at this and ask him why he wanted to talk to her.

"Strictly speaking, this is none of my business," he said. "You will probably realise that I have been talking to Jim ever since that dramatic visits of yours to Fallowfield. I am growing quite concerned. I think he is not himself at the moment."

He explained that in the course of several conversations with Jim he had noticed a growing tendency towards depression which he felt compelled to conceal. Bernard realised that learning some of the fundamental truths about his own father must have come as a real shock. Discovering he also had a brother half his own age must also have been hard. Jim must have known that his parents' marriage was unhappy, but he had managed somehow to push it, together with the dreadful trauma of their deaths to the back of his memory. The Fallowfield trip had awakened all those bad memories. Being a kind man at heart, Jim had tried to hide all this from his wife who, it seemed, had troubles of her own.

"As I said," said Bernard, "this is not really any of my business, but I am very concerned that an old friend should be suffering. You have every right to tell me to mind my own business. Is there any way in which I can help you? Brushing dirt under carpets is never a good thing, especially if some of the dirt is organic. After a time it begins to smell and dealing with it at that stage is harder."

Gemma was unsure how to reply to this. Bernard was clearly concerned for her welfare as well as Jim's. She thanked him for his concern. She was, she said, sure that they would survive this crisis. She and Jim were always open and frank in their dealings with one another. The unpleasant revelations had obviously upset everyone, but they were old enough, and sensible enough to come to terms with them. Jim would be all right. He had agreed, as she told Bernard, to have a family Christmas. It would take a while to adjust to all the changes but she was sure everyone would settle down in time. She thanked him for his obvious concern.

It was a strange call, as disturbing as it was reassuring. So much so that when she handed the handset back to Mrs Bellingham, Gemma suggested she should take the afternoon off. Mrs Bellingham was surprised but accepted the offer.

The call had disturbed Gemma. She recognised the positive motivation that had prompted Bernard Jenkins to make the call, but she was in no way grateful. There was an unpleasant feeling of resentment, when she did not at first identify, then, being honest as usual, she realised that she was angry. This was doubly confusing. The old teacher was clearly trying to be helpful and the logical reaction should have been gratitude. Instead Gemma felt angry and deeply resentful. She lay on the couch and reasoned it out. Before the visit to Fallowfield life had been relatively calm and generally pleasant. The Reunion had been explosive. The revelations of Jim's past life before Gemma met him had caused enormous upheaval. There were two aspects to this upheaval. The first, the more obvious of the two, was the extraordinary relationships that have existed more than 25 years ago. Jim's parents, whom Gemma had never known, had, it seemed, been ill matched and quite likely unfit to bring up any children. It seemed likely, too, that the cause of this was almost certainly true that Jim's father's behaviour was immoral and unacceptable. Gemma had been totally unaware of the misery which Jim must have suffered. It was incredible that he had emerged as he had, seemingly unscathed. Certainly, when Gemma had first met him, he was a rather serious, even solemn young man. It was, she recalled, she who had encouraged him to enjoy the more frivolous aspects of life as a student. Now she realised she had never really known him. In a sense, therefore, the entire married life was built on a kind of misconception. It would have been so much better had the lies never being revealed, but they had been. The cork had been removed from the bottle and the genie had escaped. No one could put it back.

She got up and made herself a hot drink. The second consequence of the visit to Fallowfield and the Reunion had been the change it had affected in Jim. He was now being forced to confront his past and he clearly was finding it difficult. It has not helped that Gemma herself was undergoing changes which affected her moods. They were slowly beginning to work towards a better understanding, but it was never the same as it had been. They had lived 20 years in a state of denial or rather of ignorance. Ignorance was best. Jim it was who had voiced his fear that Gemma was thinking of leaving. She had not seriously considered that, being far too preoccupied with her own problems, but now, in the quietness of their own home, she lay on the couch and wondered. She wondered if there was anything that could be salvaged from the years spent living a kind of lie. She wondered too if it could be possible to create a new relationship. The revelations of the past few weeks had changed both of them. The Jim she had fallen in love with was not the same man.

She was exhausted and fell into an uneasy sleep. When she woke at last, the room was dark. Jim was not due back until the morning. She took a bath, but it did not offer comfort. Instead, she found herself thinking, suicidal thoughts: how easy it would be to slip under the water and not re-emerge. She got out of the bath hurriedly, dried herself, trying to ignore the image in the mirror. She knew her body was beginning to show signs of ageing. She put on a bath robe, went down to the kitchen hoping that the bright lights would wake up change her mood, She prepared herself a simple meal and longed for someone to talk to, someone other than Jim. She could think of no one. The nearest she had to a close friend was now Sophie, but she did not want to allow her new found friend to see this deep unhappiness. For the first time in her adult life she regretted the decision she and Jim had made not to have children.

She turned on the television set but its brash cheerfulness grated on her. She was beginning to feel angry with herself. She went back upstairs and threw on some outdoor clothing. It had begun to rain. She left the lights on in the house and set off walking with no sense of direction. She passed a few houses in which the windows glowed yellow, but on the footpath which led across the common there was very little light. She walks like someone taking very deliberate exercise until she grew tired and turned back

The following morning she rang the GP surgery and made an appointment. The earliest available slot was two weeks later. Jim came home but was as preoccupied with his work as she was with her depression. He was unaware that she was going through a crisis. Gemma, nevertheless, was very slightly comforted that there was someone else in the house, especially at night. Her own behaviour began to frighten her.

Her GP was sympathetic. She would refer her for talking therapy but it would be some time before that could happen. For the time being she could only offer pills. They would help with her feelings. She recommended plenty of exercise and socialising. Meanwhile, the Hormone Replacement treatment should and would control the physical problems a little better. It was unusual, said the doctor, that the menopause had begun so suddenly and dramatically. Perhaps she would have been better at work after all.

Christmas was coming. The prospect of entertaining Sophie and Damien gave Gemma a form of distraction. She was uncertain about the plan, especially how the two men would get along. She was not too worried about Damien, but she could not be sure Jim would be willing to make a positive effort. She grew steadily more nervous as time passed. Fortunately, Sophie was as determined as she was that the venture would be a success and they spent several hours on the telephone planning in detail. It would be a novel Christmas for Gemma as well as for Sophie. Accustomed to spending the holiday in a hotel, Gemma had never bought or collected decorations, not even a Christmas tree. Furthermore, the question of presents might have been an embarrassing one, not only because the couples did not know one another that well, but also because Sophie and Damien were not as well off as Gemma and Jim. The two women agreed that presents would be restricted to two per recipient, one to be opened on Christmas morning and another in the afternoon after lunch. Although, technically, Gemma was the host they also agreed to take alternative days to organise them. The two women would work in the kitchen together on Christmas eve, preparing much of the food in advance. Christmas lunch would be followed by a collection of games which Sophie would bring with her. Boxing Day would be Gemma's responsibility and she promised to organise a visit to the sales. The following day Gemma had reserved as a special treat for her friend, but she did not disclose in advance the nature of the treat. It would involve the two women being away all day. The men would have to find something to entertain themselves. Jim was disconcerted when his wife told him he would have to find a suitable Christmas tree and set it up indoors. When Damien and his mother arrived, all four of them would set about decorating the tree. All this planning seemed to Gemma to be perfectly reasonable, though Sophie grew steadily more nervous as the holiday approached.

"Good God!" Damien exclaimed. He had stopped his old car at the entrance to the driveway. Now he and his mother sat and stared at the house before them. It was a well established, double fronted house, contrasting strongly with their own small flat. The drive curved through a well-tended lawn as far as the front door. Damien gulped and gave his mother a meaningful glance before driving the remaining yards to the main door. Gemma must have been watching out for them. She opened the door before they reached it.

"Welcome!" she said. "Do you need a hand to unload?"

They certainly did. They had two, small suitcases and one or two bags, but the back seat of the car was taken up by cardboard boxes containing various board games which had been discussed on the telephone. There was also an open box containing decorations, tinsel, and baubles to decorate the tree. Gemma called for reinforcements and Jim helped carry all this. He looked at the car and suggested Damien should take it round the back. "The tradesmen's entrance?" Damien joked. Jim did not smile.

Conversation was a little stilted Nobody felt quite at ease but they were busy, once they had spent a short time in the kitchen drinking tea. In the sitting room they admired the tree which Jim had provided. It stood in one corner, awaiting their attention. Sophie's decorations were accepted gratefully, but Jim had also spent a lot of money buying brand-new lights and large baubles. Damien sorted out the lights and at last the tree was dressed. They sat and admired it for a while. Back in the kitchen, Gemma served salad together with a quiche prepared, she explained, by Mrs Bellingham. Jim uncorked some wine.

"As soon as you two have finished breakfast," Gemma said on Christmas Eve morning, "leave the two of us to work here and amuse yourselves in the drawing room. We'll bring you some coffee later"

The two men did as she asked. The room felt a little strange to Jim, although he was the one who had bought the tall tree which felt out of place in the otherwise immaculate room. Mrs Bellingham would doubtless be put out by the pine needles which clogged the Hoover. She could hardly complain, however, in view of her generous Christmas box. The tree made Jim feel uncomfortable. It was out of place and continued to surprise him every time he came in. He did not like surprises. Nor was he fond of the tabby kitten which tried constantly to snatch the decorations from the lower branches and threatened to bring the entire structure crashing down. The cat was a recent innovation by Gemma who wanted company now she was at home all day, but Jim's protests had been overruled. He argued that a cat would hunt the birds in the garden. Damien found the cat amusing. The smart and ostentatious baubles Jim had bought were mixed with a weird collection of smaller ornaments Sophie and her son had brought with them. Jim thought of Damien as 'Sophie's son', unable even to contemplate him as his brother.

"I've been told," he announced, "that I should get to know you."

There was no obvious answer to this.

"Do you have any hobbies?" Jim asked.

"Hobbies?" Damien repeated.

"Yes, sport, clubs, activities, things like golf, bird watching perhaps?"

Damien looked at the older man, unable to answer. "No," he said finally, "nothing like that."

"Well, you must do something other than work all the time?"

"I don't have much time now I have the new job," he said. "I used to work behind the bad in the local pub but I've given that up."

"Pretty boring, is it?"

"What, the job?"

"That too. I meant life in general."

"Boring? Good God, no. I love it. I spend all my time surrounded by intelligent young people."

"Doing what?"

"Talking mostly."

"Talking?"

Damien nodded. "Most of the time."

Jim wandered aimlessly round the room as though looking for inspiration. Damien watched hm. He saw a middle-aged man with whom he had nothing in common. This was worse than a job interview. He wished he had his laptop with him. He wondered if Jim would be especially offended or annoyed if he played a game on his phone. Maybe not.

"What about friends?" Jim asked. "Friends, girlfriends, or should I ask about boyfriends?"

"Are you saying you think I'm gay?"

"No, not exactly."

"What exactly are you asking? You sound like an old-fashioned father, asking a suitor if he's a suitable match for his daughter. I'm not your son and you're not my father and in any case you have no daughters, so why the interrogation?"

"It's not an interrogation," Jim protested. "I'm only following instructions, getting to know you."

"It feels like an interrogation. And isn't that what the Nazis said?"

"The Nazis? What are you talking about? You're too young to talk about the Nazis."

"Didn't most of them try to explain their behaviour that way at the Nurenburg Trial?"

"What in God's name are you talking about? Are you saying I'm a Nazi?"

"Are you suggesting I'm gay?"

Jim had lost the thread of the conversation. Indeed, he was far from sure there was a thread. One this was certain; he had learned nothing about this young man except that he was determined to be uncooperative or maybe he was a little mad. The conversation was not going well.

Jim left the room and Damien, idle, turned on his phone and exchanged texts with a couple of friends. ' Strange Xmas' he typed, 'Can't wait to get home.' But that was still at least three days in the future. He got up and headed for the conservatory and thence to the garden. This too was exceptionally well ordered as though all the plants and shrubs were under control, like soldiers under orders, standing to attention. Damien began to smile broadly as a mental picture formed in his mind of liveried gardeners painting the roses, as in Alice in Wonderland.

It was at this very moment that Jim emerged from behind a diamond-shaped bit of topiary. Seeing the young man smiling inanely and staring into space, Jim was unnerved. The man really was unhinged, he thought.

"What's so funny?" he asked.

"I was just wondering if you paid your gardener to paint the roses."

Jim, who had never read Lewis Carol, frowned. "No, " he said. "I believe he sprays them."

This, to his consternation, resulted in spontaneous guffaws. Jim turned away and headed indoors.

When Gemma entered the drawing room later with a tray bearing fresh coffee and biscuits, she found her husband alone. He was consulting one of his bird books.

"Where's Damien?" she asked as she put the tray down.

"No idea," said Jim. "Somewhere in the house."

"His coffee will get cold."

"He's maybe upstairs," Jim said.

"Have you had a decent chat?"

"Not really. I think he may be a little mad, to tell you the truth."

"What?"

"I can't explain. You watch him, see what you think."

"What are you talking about?"

"I found him grinning like a crocodile in the garden and, when I asked what was so funny, he said something about paying gardeners to paint the roses. I said the gardener sprayed them and he walked away in fits of laughter."

Gemma knew her husband had a limited capacity for humour and he looked quietly disturbed by what he described.

"There has to be more to it than you say," she said. "Can you give him a call, please? We're very busy in the kitchen. Oh, I forgot, pour a little milk into a saucer for the kitten."

"Cow's milk is not good for cats," Jim told her retreating back. Then he stood at the bottom of the wide staircase and called to advise his younger brother there was coffee waiting. It was almost cold so Damien took it to the kitchen to warm it in the microwave. After that the two men hardly spoke until they were summoned to the dining room for lunch. This was a surprise for Jim. He and Gemma never used the dining room. It was quite austere normally but Gemma had asked Mrs Bellingham to brighten the room as far as she could before she disappeared for Christmas. From somewhere the housekeeper had unearthed crystal candlesticks and the room was now more welcoming.

"We have done well, haven't we?" Gemma said turning to Sophie for confirmation. Sophie, her mouth full of a still warm bread roll which they had baked between them, nodded.

"I think we could all do with some fresh air later," Gemma continued, "I suggest we all go on a walk. Give us another hour."

It was a good idea. Wrapped up warmly against the cold, they walked to the end of the road, a matter of a few yards, then took a familiar footpath. It led them along the edge of a field and so to woodland. Damien enjoyed the exercise but Gemma noticed that he made no attempt to engage Jim in conversation. The older man had brought his binoculars with him and was happy to spend time looking for birds. They were not too numerous at this time of year, but Jim seemed perfectly happy to spot occasional, brown or grey traces movements in the trees. Sophie was enjoying a new landscape in company with her new friend. She and Gemma were in good spirits: their friendship was blooming.

Christmas Day was a little strange for all of them. The kitchen was now back in use. They enjoyed a late and leisurely breakfast and exchanged small gifts. The men had both needed help from the women to choose suitable gifts,, but they appeared to be successful. The women had what Sophie called "smellies". The kitten played with the discarded paper. Damien was delighted with a pair of driving gloves which he took outside to his car, partly because he wanted to turn the engine over, partly because he simply wanted a little time on his own. At Sophie's suggestion, they watched some of the festivities on television. Time passed until Gemma announced that it was time to check on the dinner, leaving Jim on his own. He promptly turned off the television and took up position in the conservatory, looking out into the garden. He was bored.

The afternoon "entertainment", it had been agreed, would be down to Sophie and her son. They brought in the large pile of board games which they had brought with them, but neither Jim nor Gemma showed much enthusiasm about learning any of the new games. Monopoly they all agreed would take too long. Trivial Pursuit kept them moderately happy for one hour, but it was a well thumbed pack of playing cards which proved the most popular. By early evening they were all getting bored.

"You two," Sophie said, addressing Jim and Damien, "are a bit of a disappointment, aren't you?"

Jim took this as a criticism of himself, as indeed it was.

"We haven't exactly come to blows," he protested.

"You haven't really got to know one another, either."

"To be fair," said Damien, "there is a big age difference. You three were all born at around the same time. I am a whole generation behind you. It's not surprising we seem to have very little in common. You didn't even have mobile phones when you were my age."

That, they had to admit, was true, a valid point.

"But at least you shared the same father," Gemma insisted.

"Well, no, we didn't," Damien corrected her. "I never met him, remember. Until very recently I had no idea who he was. I'm not sure that I want to know, from what you've told me."

Jim nodded agreement. "I'm the only one here who knew him – well, apart from you, Sophie, but you must have seen him through rose coloured spectacles, and you were very young at the time. I grew up with him and I had a miserable time of it. You had a lucky escape, Sophie, as I see it. He and my mother were always quarrelling. I imagine he was probably philandering much of the time. He was never kind to me or my mother"

"That's all very well," Damien said, "but I grew up completely without a father. Okay, so mum did a pretty good job. I'm not complaining, but I didn't have a father to take part in the parents' races or even to attend parents' evenings. But that's another thing you may find difficult to understand: it's quite common these days to grow up in a family without a father. I don't know if that was a good thing or not. All I know is I didn't really miss him."

"What I suppose I was hoping for," Gemma said, "was that you two would become friends. After all, you share a lot of genes in common."

The two men looked at one another. They had not really thought in those terms.

After a while Damien said, "What if the genes we share turned out to be the bad ones? Did you ever consider that?"

Gemma looked shocked. It had not crossed her mind.

"I never thought of it," she said. "Remember, I never knew Jack. Jim and I only met after he had died and we didn't discuss him."

They were silent after this. The day had turned sour. They watched as the kitten continued to scurry about among the scraps of paper and ribbon.

"Some bloody Christmas!" Jim muttered.

There were one or two attempts after that to begin less intense conversations. But the mood was now an unhappy one. When Gemma went out to the kitchen to tidy away the remains of the meal, Sophie followed her. They worked together without speaking at first, then Sophie said all at once, "You know subconsciously I may have been seeing Jim as a kind of substitute father. I have always been very aware, ever since we met you, that he and Damien are really two different generations, although they both had the same father."

Gemma stopped what she was doing and sat down.

"And I wonder if I might have had some idea of adopting a ready-made son. Once or twice lately I have had the odd twinge of regret that we have no children. Jim and I decided that many years ago and we've never discussed it again. I suppose it's the menopause."

Sophie looked at her, surprised but with compassion. "You have only one life," she said, "and it's so easy to mess it up – not that you have messed it up, I don't mean that. We all take decisions we regret. I suppose the best we can do is learn to live with them and concentrate on the good consequences. Regrets get you nowhere. Deciding to keep Damien when I was only 16 was one such decision and certainly limited my life, but I honestly have never once regretted it."

"Who would choose to be a woman, eh?" Sophie commented and the two women smiled at one another.

"Anyway," Sophie said, "Damien is my son. I'm afraid you can't have him. I don't suppose I shall have him to myself much longer. He's longing to get away, be on his own, and who can blame him?"

"As for your "good consequences"," Gemma said, "you are absolutely right. We decided not to have children but to remain free to develop our own careers. I suppose we have done that, though neither of us was truly ambitious. I didn't want to be a highflying lawyer, dashing around in a smart suit from country to country, and I can't see Jim as a highflying diplomat or something. But we have got this house and a very comfortable standard of living."

"It certainly looks like that," said Sophie.

"Oh dear! I didn't mean…"

"Don't worry, I know what you meant. And I don't altogether envy you, but notice that little word altogether. Of course I love this house."

"Which reminds me," said Gemma, "the reason I wanted you to stay on until the 27th of the month, was that you and I are going to have a special day out together. The plan was to leave the men to do something together as well. Do you think they will want to?"

"Who knows? Who cares? They can go their own separate ways if they want to. They are both grown-ups."

For some reason this made them both laugh and they were still laughing a few minutes later when they rejoined the men.

They had decided that Boxing Day would not be spent in the house. The sales were on. After breakfast all four of them drove into town where the women looked for bargains. They had a light snack in a café. The crowds were busy, jostling, enjoying themselves. Everywhere they looked there were people carrying large paper bags full of purchases. By mid afternoon feet were beginning to feel sore and, seeing the local cinema was showing a film that appealed to all of them, like badly behaved schoolchildren they made their way noisily into a back row and watched a completely forgettable comedy. They found the car and went home to a meal of leftover turkey. There was no more serious talking and they were all happy to have an early night.

When Gemma and Jim had planned the few days they were to share with Sophie and her son, it had been agreed that Gemma's Christmas present to her new friend would be a full day at a spa. It would be an unusually expensive treat, although Gemma was unsure if Sophie would want the attentions of a rival hairdresser. She would in any case enjoy the pedicure, manicure, facial, and a full body massage. As for the men, Jim had actually put some thought into this. Knowing that Damien was a relatively new driver, he had arranged a visit to a racing circuit some distance away. He did not tell the younger man where they were going, merely settling him into the passenger seat of his very comfortable car and driving away. The experience for Damien was a mixture of exhilaration and terror. Even driving around the circuit at a modest speed was a challenge in a car which responded like a thoroughbred to every command. With the professional driver at his side the final part of the experience was to drive at speed. When at last he stopped the car for the last time, he was not sure that he had enjoyed the experience. He had never been so terrified in his life. He was very happy for Jim to drive home as his heart rate gradually slowed and his breathing became normal. By the time they reached home he thought he had enjoyed it after all and he was secretly proud to have completed the course. For his part, Jim, who had begun the exercise simply as a host looking after a visitor, found he experienced unaccustomed, paternal feelings towards the young man. He was baffled by his own reaction, finding he felt protective towards this young man and wanted him to do well.

As Damien drove his mother home the following day, neither of them wanted to talk. All in all, it had been a successful holiday after all. There would doubtless be more discussion in the future. While Sophie had found a soulmate in Gemma, the relationship between the two men was still not entirely untroubled. Damien had slipped into a bookshop on Boxing Day and, as they began their journey home, he had handed Jim a brightly tired package. When Jim went back indoors and opened it, he found a small book, "Alice's adventures in Wonderland". Damien had written a very short dedication on the flyleaf: "Please note this was written before the invention of spray paint." Sophie, in the passenger seat, was remembering the wonderful massage. She felt her entire body was glowing. She would have to start work again in the morning but that still seemed a long, long way ahead.

Chapter Five

Mentally, as the New Year arrived, and Jim began the busy time of the year, when all his clients were anxious to get their tax returns completed before the deadline, he and Gemma would take time to settle. Their brains were like concert harps which someone had accidentally stumbled into. The strings still vibrated and reverberated unharmoniously. Gemma was used to this annual pressure on Jim. This year she was not sorry that he would be preoccupied. It would give her time to sort her our own problems. But life, she was about to be reminded, did not always stick to routine.

Jim plunged into his work. From experience he knew that he would have no time to himself before the end of January. Indeed, for most of the month he would be working much of the night as well as the day. Damien was back in college and he, too, expected to spend most nights at work. For Sophie January was less busy. Most of her customers had been eager to get their hair done before Christmas, but there was still some to keep her busy. Even Mrs Bellingham was driven to work harder than usual, having had a few days off to look after her own family. She began a methodical spring cleaning of the large house. This unsettled Gemma who did not feel quite fit enough to return to her full-time job. Instead she volunteered for a couple of charities. It ensured that she spent some time most days out of the house and kept her in contact with other people. On the occasional day when she felt mentally foggy, she could thus take time off with a fair conscience. In this way time sped by.

The pressure had barely eased the first week of February when Mrs Bellingham signed for an official-looking letter addressed to Jim. He had been visiting a client all day. Gemma found the brown envelope in the kitchen where they would eat a meal together. She drew her husband's attention to it. He picked up at knife and slit open the envelope. He had noted an official logo, not one he was familiar with, for "Marchand and Butterworth, solicitors". He assumed this would be an official letter to do with one of his clients. He would take it up to his office and deal with it in the morning once he had scanned the first paragraph or two. However, he did not put the paperback inside the envelope. He stared at it intently, so intently that Gemma noticed. His face expressed shock.

"Bad news?" she asked.

"The worst. It's Bernard Jenkins. Heart attack. He died on Saturday." His voice was shaking.

"I'm so sorry," Gemma said. "You were very fond of him, won't you?"

Jim did not trust himself to reply and Gemma was disturbed to see him cry. It was Sandra's but uncontrollable. The news had not just upset him, it had shaken him to the core. Gemma felt unable to console him. Once, perhaps, she would have put her arms round him to comfort him but their relationship had become formalised and awkward. She could do little other than turn away.

He explained that the letter was signed by a limited Marchand. It explained that Bernard Jenkins had not only been a client for more than 40 years, he was also a close, personal friend. The letter pointed out that some months earlier Bernard had spoken to Leonard Marshall and made an unusual request which was only partially explained in his well. It would, said Marshall, the necessary for him to speak in person to Jim. He realised that the information will be a shop, that he understood there had been a close relationship between Jim and Bernard. He wanted to carry out Bernard's wishes, although there were only partly formed. Please call and let the solicitor know when it might be convenient to discuss the matter. He would happily drive to meet him.

"It's a very strange letter for a solicitor," Gemma commented.

"I suppose it is. It seems to hint at some kind of legacy bequest. I don't really want any money. I neither he left it to a good cause, one he cared about and one which needs the money more than we do."

The following day Jim rang Leonard Marshall. It was a brief conversation in which the solicitor explained very little, saying it was quite complicated. He agreed to drive to meet Jim two days later.

Leonard Marchand was a well preserved octogenarian. He wore a three-piece suit, immaculately cut. He stepped out of his shiny car and extended well manicure hand to Jim.

"Thank you for allowing me to come to see you," he said. "I hope you will find it will be time well spent. You will understand the delicate nature of my mission better if I explain it in person."

"I am intrigued," Jim said, leading the way indoors, "what is so important that it brings you all the way from Fallowfield."

Marchand followed him into the drawing room and arranged himself gracefully on the large sofa. Gemma, who had been ensconced in an armchair, smiled at the newcomer and prepared to leave.

"Mrs Grainger," the solicitor said, "unless your husband has any objections, I think it would be very good for you to participate in the discussion."

Gemma and Jim explained glances. Jim shrugged and his wife resumed her position in the easy chair.

"Forgive me if this explanation seems somewhat inadequate," said Marchand.

"Well, since it is obviously something to do with Bernard," Jim said, "I the only thought that has crossed my mind has been that he may have misguidedly left three some kind of bequest. If so, I don't really want it, nor do I really needed. I'd rather it went to a charity."

Marchand had put on a pair of spectacles over which she now stared at Jim. "This is not a bequest in the normal sense of the word," he said. "I told you it was complicated. Please bear with me. I believe I intimated in my letter that Bernard was not only a client of mine but he was also a personal friend. We have known each other since we were children together. His death is therefore, as a shock, but over the last few months we have been working together. Bernard, as I'm sure you must know, was very fond of you, had been ever since he first taught you in the sixth form. That must have been 30 years ago."

"He was very good to me at that time," Jim admitted. I had a very unhappy childhood. My father was a very strict man who went out of his way to make me feel a failure. Bernard Jenkins was my teacher but he was really the only adult who believed in me. Indeed I suppose I came to see him as a father rather than a teacher."

"Bernard gave me quite a lot of information on the subject," said the solicitor. "I believe he also gave you quite a lot of private tuition, free of charge, hoping to see you launched into an academic career."

Jim nodded. He had no idea where this was leading.

"Perhaps I should point out that much of the information he passed on to me of the subject was over the past year. In fact, the entire saga began for me when a former member of your year group organised a reunion."

At this both Jim and Gemma looked at the solicitor with seven, new attention.

"What you do not know, I presume, is that our mutual friend was consumed by guilt. I don't believe he discussed this with you."

"Guilt? What kind of guilt?"

"I warned you itis was complicated. The guilt I refer to dates to the time that you, your mother, and father quite suddenly left Fallowfield more than 20 years ago.

A you will not know the part that Bernard played in that move."

"Bernard? What has the to do with it?"

"I'm sure you will know the reason for that move, although you had no idea at the time. It involved the scandal and your father is part in it."

"My father," Jim admitted bitterly, "was a paedophile."

"He was never charged," said Marchant, "but a small number of his colleagues, together with the governors at the time, took the reprehensible step of getting rid of him. Bernard knew of a vacancy in the school here, where you still live. It was he that engineered a sudden discreet transfer. The scandal involving young woman called Sophie Masters, a child of 15 years. To complete the plan the Masters family – that is, Mr Masters – was given what was called a resettlement payment, enabling them to move at the same time. One consequence of this cover-up was that the break was to be absolute. Both parties, your father and the Masters, would not communicate in any way. They signed written agreements to that effect. One of the most regrettable consequences of this irregular and probably illegal arrangement was that your contact with Bernard Jenkins was also terminated. You appear to have built a successful business for yourself notwithstanding, but any plans which you were formulating with Bernard's connivance came to an end. This year the so-called reunion brought all this back to light. Hence the guilt I referred to."

Gemma looked from Leonard Marchand to her husband. She could think of nothing by way of a comment on what was such a distressing tale. She got to her feet and suggested coffee. Leonard looked at her gratefully.

"I'm sorry I had to be so explicit," he said, "but it is necessary for you to understand the purpose of my visit. I did not come merely to give you information which you may or may not already know. I came because our mutual friend, Bernard Jenkins, had been talking about this in confidence to me over the past few months. He left me with a conundrum. I very much hope that you will help me solve it."

Gemma stood up and went in search of coffee. She found Mrs Berry home in the kitchen had foreseen this and laid a tray in readiness. Back in conference mode, the solicitor resumed.

"Bernard's untimely death," he said has left me with a very difficult task, one which is not only difficult but delicate. He was hoping to atone for his behaviour and so at least to appease the guilt I have described. The discovery of your half brother, Damien, which must have come as a considerable shock also appeared to Bernard to offer an opportunity."

"An opportunity? How did you work that out? The boys half my age. He might be good at maths, but I can't see how his existence is going to make up for the disruption to my education. I even have my doubts about his sanity, but that maybe because he belongs to a different generation. What on earth did Bernard have in mind?"

"Well, among other things, there is the matter of his estate."

"What estate?"

"It consists mainly of his house. It could probably do with a little refurbishing, but it is worth a substantial amount. He was so uncertain what to do about it that he thought me to draw up a new will. He did not know how to divide the estate between the two of you."

"I told you," said Jim, "I don't want any of his money."

Gemma and Leonard Marchand looked at him.

"The situation at present," said Marchand, "is this: at Bernard's suggestion, his estate is to be held in trust until a final solution is agreed between the two brothers and myself as the executor. As I understand his instructions – and we talked about this at some length – there is to be one major condition applied to the settlement: it must in some way need to what he called a "rapprochement" between the two brothers. He felt this amazingly strongly. I'm afraid I'm out of my depth here and I really need your help. That includes you, Mrs Grainger."

At Gemma's insistence, he stayed long enough to take a bowl of soup but refused to delay long enough for coffee. Over this meagre lunch he spoke in a less formal way.

"Bernard and I," he said "were of exactly the same age. We even went to nursery school together. We were more like brothers than friends. His death comes as a considerable shock, as you may imagine. When you reach a certain age you come to accept grief as a daily companion. You look back on all life and identify the most precious moments and cherish them. Those memories are the most important part of your life, even if they are not shared with anyone else. Regrets weigh you down, hold you back, make the daily encounter with grief that much more difficult."

He took his leave, thanking them both for receiving him and repeating his hopes that they would think hard about what he called "his problem".

"What a sad old man!" Gemma said as the car left the driveway.

"Sad? Maybe. Impressive," said Jim.

Jim showed little inclination to return to his office when they had finished drinking coffee together.

"Do you have any regrets?" he asked to Gemma's surprise.

"Not really," she equivocated.

"So you do?"

"Jim, the past 20 years have been wonderful, satisfying."

"But?"

"This sounds corny. But for me the magic has gone out of it sadly. We still get on quite well, but I still remember that thrill I used to feel when you came into the room. I no longer feel quite like that."

"I'm sorry," he said. "Have I been taking you for granted too long?"

"It was not your fault," Gemma said. "I just think whatever it was just ran out of steam. The memories are still there. This year has been especially difficult."

"But there have been some very good times."

"Oh yes! Lots of very good times, positive memories, and we are still good friends, I believe."

"But there's something else, isn't there?"

Gemma was reluctant to reply.

"Ever since we've met Sophie and her son I've had moments when I regretted our decision not to have children ourselves."

Jim looked at her with concern. "It's definitely too late now," he said. "And we both agreed. We talked about it for a long, long time. When did you start thinking like this?"

"I told you, it was after we met Sophie and Damien."

Jim did not reply but Gemma watched him closely. She could not interpret his expression as it changed. She watched with apprehension as he allowed his feelings to show themselves. He looked all at once older, infinitely weary, as if the events which had followed the first visit to Fallowfield and the Reunion had destroyed his world. Gemma's heart ached for him but she could not offer him the physical comfort she once had found so straightforward.

"Oh Jim," she said miserably, "I'm so sorry. I have been no help to you when you needed me most. Most men would have given up. I'd understand if you found another woman who could offer you what I can't. It might even make me feel better if you did."

She spoke from a deep desire to help him. His reaction, however, was so unexpected and expressed with such force that she was frightened. She had never in all the years she had known him felt afraid of him, but he sat up with a face that showed such anger that instinctively and for the first time she cowered in the chair, making herself as small as she could.

"What the hell are you suggesting?" he shouted, almost spitting out the words." This isn't about sex. How can you even suggest I could look for another woman? It may be what my foul father did, but not me. When we exchanged marriage vows twenty years ago, I meant them. I thought you did, too. If I broke those vows, it would mean destroying my very being. It would not only mean betraying you. It would be a deliberate end of my integrity as a person. How dare you suggest such a thing? If you can't keep your word, who are you?"

The vehemence of his words was emphasised by his movements. He stood up, made violent gestures and then picked up the table lamp on the small table and hurled it against the wall. Gemma, terrified, watched as he slowly cooled down. The rigidity of his features eased. He was like a madman at first. After a while his voice was more normal.

"I'm sorry," he said, "but never ever suggest such a thing again. The very worst thing about the man that called himself my father was that he betrayed everybody. Worse, he betrayed himself. He gave everyone the impression they knew him, but no one did. The very idea that I might be like him, well, you see what it does to me. I am sorry if I scared you."

Gemma was still in shock. She watched as Jim, calming down further, unplugged the broken lamp before fetching a dustpan and brush. She did not trust herself to speak for some time. Jim opened the drinks cupboard and poured himself a whisky. Gemma followed suit.

"I'm sorry," she said, sitting down, "I wanted to help. I should have known better. This business has been so painful for you, I know. But one thing I must say; you are nothing like the Jack you describe. That is why I am so unhappy. You have always been a wonderful husband and I have always loved you. It's just that I have changed. I've let you down."

"I married you for better or for worse in sickness and in health," Jim said. "Maybe we shall get some of the good times back one day."

To Jim's surprise, when he went to bed, Gemma followed him and asked if she could join him. They clung together for comfort but they both felt strangely shy. The warmth, the whisky and the familiar comfort of their bodies reawakened a gentle desire. They made love for the first time in months, a long, slow love-making which eased the unusual stress of the evening.

For Gemma the hours and weeks which followed were like a fog. In her mind she replayed the scene many times. Jim's violent outburst explained much. Gemma was unable to articulate her thoughts but she knew it did not matter since she would never discuss them with anyone. Impressions swirled in the fog and occasionally condensed into identifiable feelings rather than thoughts. Principle among them was the recognition that Jim's most intimate motivation was based on fear, the fear that his psyche held a dark secret, inherited from his father. All his adult life he had been haunted by this fear, afraid that one day it would grow like a cancer. Gemma sensed that her husband had always been dependent on her to provide reassurance. He knew he behaved like a decent man but he needed her to reflect back to him the image she had of him. Without her this cancer could grow. Gemma now saw him in a new light, felt deeply sorry for him, ready to help in any way she could.

Superficially life was largely unchanged, although they both knew a barrier of some kind had been broken. The old warmth returned to their relationship. They resumed their normal routines and habits, though Gemma was still not ready to return to full-time work at the office. Her charity work continued. Neither of them discussed the matter which Mr Merchant had spoken of, nor did Gemma speak to Sophie for several weeks. She needed the fog to clear a little and she was far from prepared to discuss the solicitor's request. It was Sophie who rang her.

"Are you all right?" she asked. "We haven't been in touch for weeks. I hope you're not ill."

"No, I'm fine. I have just been a bit preoccupied of late. How are you?"

"Fine. Nothing much to report. Businesses much the same, doing okay. Damien seems to have settled into his new job by now. He has found himself a new girlfriend, a nice girl called Carol. It had to happen sooner or later, but I'm already beginning to feel it difficult. I shall no longer be the centre of his universe. I must try not to make him the centre of mine."

"So, it's good news in some ways and not so good in others."

"That's life. I'm sure we'll cope. By the way I never thank you properly for that day at the spa. I still think about it when I feel a bit low. It was wonderful."

"Glad you enjoyed it. Pity we didn't get to the brothers to get together better."

"I suppose it's not surprising. 25 years is a long time. They don't seem to have all that much in common."

"Do you know, in a sense, I think Jim might be a little scared of getting too close."

"Scared? Why scared?"

"It sounds ridiculous, but he's worried that paedophilia could be inherited."

"Well, that really is ridiculous! Damien has been too busy to have serious girlfriends until his twenties!"

"I know. He seems to see Jack's behaviour as a kind of disease, one that can be inherited. Finding Damien appears to have started all this up again."

Sophie could think of nothing sensible to say in reply to this.

"What are we going to do about Mr Marchand's problem?" Gemma insisted.

"I really haven't a clue."

"It does seem ridiculous," said Gemma. "Jim has seen the house. Have you? It's a bit old-fashioned, as you would expect, but it would be worth quite a bit. It would be good to come up with some constructive ways to use the money, but for the life of me I can't think of how we can use it to bring Damien and Jim together."

"I don't suppose the money could be donated to another charity?"

"I shouldn't think so."

"Gemma, are you sure you're okay?"

"Yes, I'm fine. Why are you asking?"

"You sound different."

"Different? In what way?"

"You sound – relaxed – no, more contented – oh, I can't explain. You sound sort of happier somehow."

"I told you, I'm fine. Look, we really have to come up with some ideas about this weird trust idea. Can we get together? I can drive down to Fallowfield. It would be good to meet Damien's girlfriend and maybe Damien himself might have some ideas. I could even work my magic on Jim, perhaps, get him to come down as well. He is not so busy these days. In fact, we could arrange a full-scale conference and get Mr Marchand along as well. The more the merrier. What do you think?"

"Lovely idea! If we made it at the end of term, Damien might be able to find a bit more time. Do you want me to ask him?"

"Yes, let's go for it!"

Gemma turned off her phone. She felt suddenly determined and more energetic than she had been for weeks. She would introduce the idea to Jim over dinner. She began by planning the meal.

The two women worked hard and their telephone conferences resumed on an almost daily basis. They organised the conference at the end of March. It required lots of effort and tact to get everyone to commit to meeting. It would be held in Fallowfield in Mr Marchand's offices. There was, he explained, a comfortable boardroom they could use. He was taken aback when Gemma explained that they would prefer not to make the meeting too formal, and that it might be better if he were not to chair the meeting himself she got her own way. Jim had been reluctant from the start, but Gemma steered him gently, like someone guiding a blind man by the arm. Damien had expected difficulties finding a free day, but got there in the end. His girlfriend, Carol, surprised by the invitation but intrigued, was less of a problem. Sophie found the whole business exciting.

"Carol who?" Jim said.

"Carol Fairbrother, she is Damien's girlfriend. He insisted she should come. I really don't know what is the matter with you two. You both seem interested only in creating problems."

"This business has nothing at all to do with Carol whatever her name is. I wonder if he has to be there at all."

"I told you, Jim, your precious brother will only attend a meeting if she comes as well. You both seem determined to make this difficult."

Jim looked at his wife and shrugged. "So be it!" He said.

And the preliminary meeting was arranged. Jim, Gemma, Sophie, Damien, Damien's girlfriend, and Leonard Marchand were welcomed into the gloomy boardroom. They took their places at one end of the large table. Mr Marchand reminded them what the purpose of the meeting was. He explained that he had been asked by his old friend to use the proceeds of his estate in some unspecified way to help Jim and Damien to find some way of working together, maybe setting up a project of some kind. The estate consisted largely of a fair sized house which could be sold together with its contents. It would be worth somewhere in the region of £850,000. He, the executor of the estate, had so far been unable to suggest the project which would satisfy the demands of his old friend. If, he said, they could suggest a suitable project, he would be happy to set up a small, charitable organisation. Not including himself, there were just enough people to set up a formal committee. The problem was finding a suitable project.

No one replied. It was, Jim thought, rather like a hand of breach when nobody wanted to start the bidding. There were several minutes of embarrassed silence which drove Gemma to make the first suggestion. Instead of selling the house, why not use it for some kind of community work, a place where people could gather and pursue their hobbies. The idea was shot down in flames almost immediately. A modified suggestion from Sophie was that the building could be used as a youth centre. This, too, was short lived. Mr Marchand pointed out in his polite but firm voice that retaining the building would incur running costs. It would be better to sell and to use the money as Bernard Jenkins had indicated. He reminded everybody that the sale of the building and its contents would yield only a modest amount. There was another long period of silence.

"Could the money be used to help would-be students in some way?" Carol asked. "Some would-be students, even budding mathematicians, are put off from applying for university courses when they really only need a very small amount. Small grants of, say, £500 could make all the difference in some cases. I know that Damien is very interested in promoting education and I suspect that Mr Grainger," she indicated Jim, "might share some of his enthusiasm."

"Good idea!" said Jim. He gave the idea a thumbs up sign.

"It's a project we could certainly explore," said the solicitor. "Of course funds will be restricted and would most likely run out in the short time."

"I have had a little experience of similar, welfare schemes," Jim said. "What's Carol is suggesting is a charitable trust. It would be governed by all the safeguards that applied to financial procedures, even though it would necessarily be on a small scale. However, we could explore two further aspects of this: either we could donate the funds to a similar charity or we could explore ways in which to express expand the capital. Crowd funding, for example, might be one way."

Gemma was looking at her husband with admiration. All at once he was revealing skills she not seen. Opposite him Damien was nodding approval. Mr Marchand looked round summed up. There would be a great deal of work to set this up, he pointed out, but since everybody seemed to be in agreement, he proposed a preliminary organisation might be the outcome. Jim Grainger's experience in such matters and is, if she agreed, Carol's enthusiasm might be a valuable combination.

He proposed that the two of them should work with him in the first instance to sketch out the main principles and purposes of such a trust fund. Meanwhile, if everybody present agreed, as sole executor of Bernard Jenkins' will, he would begin by selling the house and contents. He proposed a meeting of Carol, Jim and himself in one month's time. By then a few details will have become clearer, including the market value of the property and the implications of seeking to expand the funds of the trust to be set up.

Mr Marchand had arranged for a buffet lunch in one of the other rooms in this ancient building. It was furnished as a waiting-room with comfortable chairs and occasional tables. Two of Marchand's assistants offered everybody hot or cold drinks.

"Thank you for your suggestion," Jim said to Carol. "I don't think any of us had a clue what to do. I didn't really know why you were here, to tell the truth."

"I was really being nosy," she said. "I'm reading law so, when Damon told me about this, I thought it would be interesting to see how an idea can be turned into a practical organisation. I didn't intend to contribute."

"But I'm glad you did," Jim said.

Damon, standing at her elbow, smiled broadly. "Clever you," he said.

Jim looked down at the wine glass in his hand. He was hiding his own smile as he recognised Damon's awkwardness. He was beginning to recognise barely remembered experiences of his own youth. He would he knew, enjoy working on this project. Perhaps his brother was not, after all, quite mad. He certainly approved of his choice of girlfriend.

Back at home Gemma refrained from discussing this strange sequence of events. She and Sophie talk to one another on the phone. They hope that this proposal to set up a trust would help to bring the two brothers together but they were far from certain how it would work, especially since the original work was to be done not with Damien but with Carol, a comparative stranger. They could only hope.

Chapter Six

One month elapsed and Jim set off early in the morning to drive to Fallowfield. He did not expect there had been much development as yet; it would take a while to sell the house, but he hoped that Carol would have produced some interesting ideas. He realised that the proposed trust deed to be clearly defined and Carol's proposal to seek crowdfunding to boost funds for the trust were outside his experience. He would find it all quite interesting and novel. It never occurred to him that participating in this scheme might be a way in which he would have to work closely with Damien. In this respect the hopes and expectations of Sophie and Gemma were completely misplaced.

He was, therefore, surprised when he met Carol again an hour before the appointed time for the meeting with the solicitor.

"Mr Grainger," Carol began, "do you mind if I ask a few personal questions?"

"That depends on the nature of the questions."

"Well," Carol said, "it's to do with you and Damien. I get the impression that other people, especially Sophie and your wife, see this project as some way to bring the two of you closer together. I understand that you have not had very much to do with one another. I also know that you and Damien did not know of one another's existence until recently."

"Go on."

"I am closer to Damien in age and we are friends. As I understand it, he is much younger than you."

"Yes, 25 years younger."

"I think Damien finds it very difficult to see you as his brother. Whatever the Sophie and your wife may feel, I think the age gap between you is going to make it almost impossible for you to develop the kind of natural relationship you expect between brothers."

"You are absolutely correct," said Jim. "This whole business has made me aware what different worlds we live in. To be honest I don't really know how to talk to him."

"Well, I suspect that is mutual. I also think, taking your age difference into account, that Damien is more likely to see you as a kind of father figure rather than a brother."

"That had not occurred to me," Jim said.

"How would you feel about that kind of relationship?"

Jim thought for a minute. "It would make more sense," he said. "We don't have many interests in common. I don't understand his sense of humour for example."

"I get the impression that neither of you really want a close relationship, but you would be happy to be friends. There might well be occasions where he could approach you for advice. I'm not suggesting you suddenly adopt a new son. I'm not entirely sure what I am suggesting, but I think this project which we have in mind should not be seen as a means of bringing the two of you together. If that happens, that would be a kind of bonus. The whole purpose of setting up this trust fund must be to help young people who need the money."

"Do you know," Jim commented, "what you say makes a great deal of sense. I would be far happier accepting that I have a young relative who doesn't expect anything from me nor I from him. In fact the very idea leaves me with a kind of relief."

They sat for a while, both busy with their thoughts.

"You are a remarkable young woman," Jim said. Carol smiled but did not reply.

"Gemma and Sophie will just have to learn to accept the situation," Jim continued. "The mean well, but they have really been trying to – I don't know – adopt a role that neither I nor Damon really wants. I found myself quizzing him one day, asking him about his work, which I didn't understand, and even about his girlfriends. It felt wrong at the time. I think you're approach could be far better. Damon is simply a young man, half my age, with his own life to lead. We shall probably get to know one another the way that you normally get to know strangers. I'm not intensely interested in his life and I don't think he is very interested in mine, so I don't want to force the issue and a longer. But thank you for making me think about it. As I said, you really are a remarkable young woman. It's going to be a privilege to work with you."

It was time to meet Mr Marchant for the first of many meetings. The three participants, Jim realised, came from three generations: Marchand was in his late 70s, Jim was in his 40s, Carol was in her 20s. The range of experience would doubtless prove valuable.

When, much later, Jim got home, Gemma sensed a change in him. He seemed more settled, happier, with a renewed sense of purpose. It was a mood which affected her, too, as she reported to Sophie in one of their long, telephone calls. The Reunion had led to a confused and difficult year. Its effects would be long lasting and no one on could have suspected what changes had already been affected. Gemma and Jim had survived a crisis in their marriage. Sophie and Gemma had forged a very close relationship. The two brothers, separated by age, would remain aware of one another but it seemed unlikely they would form a close partnership although Carol Fairbrother had unexpectedly become an important element in the project to set up a charitable trust for would be students in the future.

That summer, at Gemma's suggestion, she and Jim chose not to take a holiday abroad. Instead they contributed the first thousand pounds to the fund. Gemma returned to work part-time. Jim continued with his usual business. He did not make a special effort to forge closer links with Daemien, though they met occasionally. Carol became a good friend and colleague. Gemma and Sophie developed their friendship. The invitation to the Reunion had disturbed all their lives, digging up the past but, one year on, it was as though the experience was like digging a garden which had lain fallow for a long time. Weeds and worms which had been buried had been brought to the surface, but the newly exposed soil began to produce fresh plants and they would doubtless grow into healthy flowers in due course.

THE END

www.ingramcontent.com/pod-product-compliance
Ingram Content Group UK Ltd.
Pitfield, Milton Keynes, MK11 3LW, UK
UKHW021942200425
457661UK00001B/44